Undead Strippers Versus The Alien Zombie Queen

By, Clayton Overstreet

The Problem

People die. It happens every day in a lot of different ways. One moment they are alive and then an accident, the ill intent of another person, or natural causes knock them out of this world.

Lorene Thomas, AKA Roxy, had in her life been personally responsible for the deaths of twenty-seven people since she was sixteen years old and was only twenty-two. The thing was, neither she nor anyone else was aware of this fact. It began shortly after she got her driver's license and a used car. Her grandparents had left her some money for it before they had been arrested. Jack and Charlene Thomas had been going down on fishing trips to Mexico for years and bringing back some real whoppers. Too bad one of the border guards had finally realized that the fish he was bringing back were not native to Mexican waters and a quick look inside showed that grandpa had been hauling more than fish. Still by then the money he had given his granddaughter was in her piggy bank at home.

Feeling good after school Lorene had gone to her the diner where her mother Darlene worked. Now Lorene had known her mother was a bit of a tramp since first grade when she had been allowed to pick out her clothes for school and had decided to dress like mommy. The teacher had immediately taken her out of class and to the principal's office where they called her mother and she had to sit there while they explained to Darlene that a low cut top, big bleach blond hair, and makeup were not appropriate for an elementary school student and why. Darlene had been outraged and tried arguing that they were unfair un calling her a "tramp" (a word Lorene had looked up in the dictionary later) but the next time she went to school Lorene had done so in a more normal pink dress.

That incident and the fact that her mother dated men who usually smelled of been and tobacco should have had her ready for anything, but as she pulled around the back of the diner she was shocked to see her single mother blowing her uncle Bobby. A horrible suspicion hit her. She had always resembled Bobby, but her mother had always said she had his nose because he was her uncle. Darlene had also been evasive on who Lorene's father actually had been. Feeling sick she had floored the accelerator and tore rubber out of there. She went home and packed a bag before taking off for New York City, never once looking back. Unfortunately in doing so she startled her mother who both bit down and gasped. When the police found the bodies the autopsies showed that Bobby Thomas had died of massive blood loss and Darlene Thomas had choked on a "foreign object".

Once in New York Lorene had found her dreams of big city living had not been as grand as she hoped and soon she had to sell most of her things including the car and take a little hole in the wall apartment. Not long after to make ends meet she had ended up turning tricks for a pimp named Juan. When she was eighteen she got another job at *Barely Legal*, a strip Club. At first she tried saving up but her boss was a cheapskate and she had to pool her tips with the other girls. So she supplemented her income by blowing guys in bathrooms as bars behind Juan's back and saving the money until she was able to get a slightly better apartment on Long Island, where she moved without telling anyone.

When she disappeared one of Juan's other ladies called Candy suspected him of having killed her and decided that if he was going to do that she would take him out. The police found him knifed in a dumpster a week later and the girls had no problem with the new management. Bolstered by this success Candy went too far and got involved with some drug runners who had been trying out new methods of transporting smack since their old mover got sent to prison when the police found the drugs inside the fish they were hauling. They tried to use her girls and one thing led to another and soon all the girls and half the syndicate were in jail or dead in a huge shoot out with the DEA.

Meanwhile Lorene, known to her friends and the arresting officers as Roxy, was scrounging a living on Long Island, locking her door on her rat hole apartment every night, afraid that Juan would track her down. She got a new job at a new strip club, what with not having any skills at anything else or a diploma. She tried to kid herself that she was saving up for college, though she kept spending money on clothes and sometimes drugs to the point where sometimes she could not afford power or even food. Until the day she blew all her savings on bigger breasts so she could earn more and admitted to herself that she was never going to have a job whose retirement plan did not revolve around an overdose of something highly illegal.

Lately though, things had been going okay for her, as far as she was concerned. The power had been out on the island for a few weeks now. Lorene took a perverse joy in everyone else knowing what it was like to live on canned food and take cold showers. There had been some sort of crash and maybe a terrorist attack of something in the middle of Long Island so there had been a lot of army guy coming through for a while, getting her extra tips at the bar and even some extra income blowing a few in an alleyway. She did not know why, not being much for newspapers and having no TV. She did not really care either. Lorene had stopped thinking much past her immediate desires a long time before.

Occasionally she thought about her life. The men who paid her to sleep with her fell into a few categories. The kind who were nervous losers who had rarely if ever been with a woman. The freaks who wanted to do something kinky that their regular women would not go for. And the ones like the army guys who were in town on business and wanted to do something that nobody would ever find out about. But then, every regular boyfriend Lorene had ever been with was the same way and in her experience they really did all just want one thing from a woman. So why not get paid for it? Besides she actually enjoyed the sex with her Johns better than all the dancing a person had to do in a relationship. If she felt like she wanted to do something kinky she did not have to work up to it, but just ask the guy and they were usually gung ho to try it.

She was beginning to get worried though. A long black out was one thing, but it was getting ridiculous and even the grocery store had closed up. The club she worked at was closed down and the other girls were gone. She was a hooker full time now and the pickings were getting mighty slim, mostly homeless people and guys in camouflage who drove around in trucks with guns. She sometimes went all night without even hearing even cars passing in the street now.

Still a girl had to eat so she put on enough makeup to make a clown jealous under her big blond hair, a yellow tube top, a belt-like leather mini-skirt that did nothing to hide her lack of panties, green fish net stockings, and a pair of neon pink platform high heeled shoes. She picked up her little spaghetti string purse and headed out. On the sidewalk outside her building she saw Jimmy, one of the last hold outs, holding a new sign. This one said, "Family Eaten By Zombies. Need Money For Shotgun Shells." Three weeks before she had slipped him two bucks because he had one that read, "My dog was kidnapped by a warlord and his samurai army. Need money for Ninjitsu classes." But this new one was ridiculous. Zombies? Like she had never seen that one before.

Walking past him she made her way to her regular alley off main street. People driving around did not like taking the freeway any more. There had been a lot of wrecks and nobody had taken them down. Heck the thing was practically barricaded from what she had heard from some people, so most of the cars detoured through town. It was her best bet.

So she leaned against her usual street light, though the only light came from the moon up above. At least there was less competition lately. Hell the place was almost a ghost town. Much more of this and she would have to blow a guy for a ride out of town so she could get some fresh prospects.

Lorene was almost ready to call it a night when a group came around the corner. Maybe six or seven people. She patted her hair, adjusted her boobs, and leaned over a bit so they could see her cleavage. "Hey, any of you up for a good time?"

They stopped, silhouettes in the dark, until one came forward. It was a young looking Japanese girl with blue hair. "Maybe we are."

"I don't do chicks," Lorene said. Sixteen years of getting up on Sunday counted for something. Besides chicks who hired hookers were clingy, like one roll with them would not only turn her gay, but make her propose and head right down to adopt seven babies. The few times she had done it always went south. "Plus you look a little young. How old are you?"

"Oh don't worry," the girl said. "I just want to watch. The boys however could use a little fun." Behind her the group moaned, groaning in unison. Except one who buttered, "Jesus Beth, seriously?" The girl ignored this and pulled out her wallet, flashing a few hundreds. "Come on, in the alleyway. I'll give you the whole wad if you take on all of them at once." She pulled out half and pressed it into Lorene's hand.

"You're not cops are you?"

"Nope."

Eying the money Lorene nodded. If they were police then that denial made it entrapment if they tried to arrest her, so she was legally covered. "You got it babe." For that much money she would bang a football team, including the coach, the water boy, and the cheerleaders.

She walked into the nearby dark alley and leaned provocatively against the high chain link fence that blocked the way through. With a deft move she hitched up her skirt and pulled down her top, squishing her breasts in her hands. "Come and get it boys!"

The girl and the guy who had spoken stayed back near the entrance, probably as look outs. Some people were cautious, lest the hooker be a cop herself or if the police happened by. Still she could make out the eager gleam on the girl's face as the other five came towards Lorene, moving slowly and groaning hungrily. These guys clearly had not been laid in a while.

Then one stumbled and Lorene saw something fall out of his pants. As he walked he kicked it towards her and it rolled down the alley ahead of them and bumped into her shoe. She looked down and saw the tube-shaped thing. A sex toy? These boys were ready to roll. Bending down she picked it up and said, "Hey you dropped…" She trailed off. The thing in her head looked like a dildo, but it felt like cold meat and when she peered closely she saw… sores? Rot? "Ew!" It was a real penis! She dropped it. "What the fuck?"

Looking up at the men who were close now, she saw them as they stepped into a patch of moonlight. Their skin was pale and rotting away. One had skull peeking through the left side, like a mask but instead of being over the skin it was in. His long purple dried out tongue stuck out of his mouth like a dog's, limp and useless. From wounds on all of them that looked like human bite marks, but with puss and black coagulated blood seeping from them.

She had no where to run and they were on her a moment later. Too strong to fight and blocking her only exit. The tiny clothes she was wearing did nothing to protect her and soon she felt their cold hands clasping her and their still sharp teeth sink into her flesh, chewing and tearing. As she sank into darkness the girl came into view. Towering behind her was something pale and inhuman. Of the two of them the monster was the one who looked sickened by her predicament. The girl looked almost sexually excited.

As if to prove the point the girl bent down and scooped up the rotten phallus that Lorene had dropped and gently tossed it in among the feasting undead. "Keep the tip." She hated to admit it, but Lorene's last thought was that the joke, sick as it was, had been pretty funny.

Briefing

At thirty thousand feet Sheila Casey was sitting in a small room in an

airplane and staring around at creatures that could only be described as

monsters. Not that they looked terrible. With a few notable differences they

all looked human enough. Someone might stare if they passed on the street,

but their first thought would not be to grab torches and pitchforks. Though it

should. They all had glasses of champagne and Sheila had a bowl of her

favorite snack, chocolate covered ants, in the middle of the table.

"You are all probably wondering why I brought you all together?" The five

women sitting at the table eyed one another and her. When they had been

"invited" on this trip by groups of armed soldiers of the black ops variety

they had not expected the young looking girl to be behind it. She was a blond Jewish girl and barely looked old enough to drive, let alone wield the kind of power that had been used to round them all up. But of all people these were the last ones to judge someone on their looks. Nobody said anything as she continued speaking with authority. "I need your help to save the world." Standing she picked up a remote for a projector. The screen behind her lit up with a map of Long Island. "You are all familiar with the fact that Long Island has been quarantined for several weeks?"

"Yeah, they said on the news it was an Ebola outbreak or something," one of them said.

"Not exactly. Truthfully the entire island is infested with what the government has been forced to classify as zombies." Nobody expressed any disbelief so she continued. "Roughly five weeks ago something crashed in a park. Something that was of extraterrestrial origin. It had two surviving passengers. A species called Mind Lords. Physically similar to large versions of our spiders, roughly two feet across and six inches high, these creatures are body snatchers originally designed by the people of their planet as biological weapons. Their creators were incurably war like, but the Mind Lords were not, so the prototypes escaped and conquered the planet, becoming useful members of galactic society. Most of them refuse to even try to take over any other species but the one from their home world for fear

13

of diseases, being trapped inside an alien body they cannot control, and also because most of them feel this is wrong.

"However there is a significant group among them who feel otherwise and want to find as many worlds to conquer as possible. They believe they are on a holy mission from God to unite all intelligent creatures and will do anything to accomplish this goal. In this instance one of them managed to infiltrate part of a deep space exploration crew as an engineer. When they approached Earth, which is supposed to be off limits, she tried to convert the mission's captain. When that failed she turned on the other Mind Lord and the resulting fight crashed the ship, killing their host bodies and leaving the captain unconscious." The women stared wide-eyed at her. One started to speak and Sheila held up a hand. "Please allow me to finish before asking questions.

"The rogue alien went in search of a host body and acquired one. The other eventually woke up and carefully tracked her, finding that she had established a connection with teenage earth girl. That left the captain alone on an alien planet with a broken ship. He returned and watched for several days as authorities came to investigate the crash. He then contacted one of them in the only way it could." She turned around and lifted up the back of her shirt. Around the room there were gasps. An impressive response when half of them did not actually need to breathe.

Sheila had a giant gray spider-like thing apparently fused to her back, its legs and other things like suction cups sunk deep into her skin. It blinked three eyes at them and its abdomen throbbed. Sheila quickly lowered her shirt and turned around, speaking in a deeper voice. "Greetings Earthlings, I am Captain Mind Ripper."

"So who is in charge?" One of the others asked.

"We… this body called Sheila and I as well as other members of this country's government… are working together to contain this problem." The voice changed back to the one she had been using before. "Yes it's a bit creepy, but I was the one the captain contacted and the only survivor of what happened next so for now the two of us are partners." Her voice changed again. "I fully intend to remove myself from this host as soon as the crisis is at an end." Sheila took control again. "But let me continue with the briefing.

"While Captain Mind Ripper spent several days observing and deciding who to try to merge with my team from the FBI were examining the space craft and something unexpected happened. A dozen or so people appeared at the perimeter of the crash site and immediately began attacking the men on guard without warning. We had been unsure if it was a model, a drone, or a real UFO. We were just sent in to determine what was going on. So there was not much security, but enough to deter most people. Mostly we put up a chain link fence and stood around while scientists examined the thing. These people were ordered to leave, but they ignored it. They continued to advance and the soldiers we brought with us from the National Guard went to remove them by force. As soon as they got close and without warning these people then attacked the guards, biting them and then coming after the rest of us. We fired on them, but it was useless and while we were running out of ammunition our guards got up and began helping attack us."

"Zombies," someone muttered.

"So we determined later. I escaped to report, but the plague spread fast and by the time help arrived and were convinced that the problem really was zombies, it was too late to stop it. Fortunately people living on the island apparently did not wait for the government to act and while some evacuated before the quarantine was fully in place, someone managed to destroy all the bridges and tunnels leading off. Fortunately it seems the zombies cannot cross the water."

"Running water affects undead of all kinds and salt will ground out zombies, removing the animating forces."

"So our resources have determined, though our superiors were unhappy with hiring Voodoo priests as consultants. Especially when said priests refuse to even try doing anything to fix it, saying that whatever dark forces were responsible were beyond them." Sheila took a deep breath. "Over the weeks since we've tried to determined the exact nature of the threat." Mind Ripper spoke up. "I have never even heard of the walking dead before this. Our species is highly scientific, barring some of our religious beliefs, and I doubt any of us would believe such a thing possible."

"Welcome to Earth," someone quipped while all five monsters smiled nastily.

Sheila cleared her throat. "I on the other hand have had personal experience with the supernatural before. Not something I shared, but once it was established that normal channels were not working I felt the need to take action."

"Normal channels?"

"Army personnel sent in. Scientists. Captured enemies studied for viral outbreak. We lost 90% of those sent to the island and the rest retreated with major casualties. Satellite observation shows that the zombies are spreading exponentially and already outnumber the humans still trapped on the island by about a thousand to one and growing. Missiles were sent in, but they have encountered some kind of shield that prevents them from working." Mind Ripper spoke up, "I suspect that Flower of the Pond has adapted the shields from my space ship to protect the island from attacks. They are designed to allow us to pass near stars and through unknown gasses, but allow us movement should we need to operate in space. Even a blast from a nuclear weapon would be absorbed easily."

"Flower of the Pond?"

"The English translation of her name. I understand it is common on Earth to not know the meaning behind one's name, but the translator I use gives the literal meaning."

"So you cannot read minds?"

"No. My control of a host extends only to the bodily processes."

Sheila held up a hand. "Questions later." The women looked like they had a lot, but they knew this was just going to get weirder so they quieted down. "The shield allows air and people to pass easily, but have strange magnetism that prevent anything made of iron and steel from going through and somehow filters out toxic gasses too. There are ceramic weapons but they are few and we are not sure we have time to get the numbers needed to be effective, though we are working on it. We assume that they don't consider humans who go to the island a threat and are willing to take as many victims as they can get to add to the horde. So far, they are right.

"Aside from the zombies we know that Flower of the Pond will likely begin working towards her people's plan of world infestation. Captain Mind Ripper assures me that his communication devices were ruined in the crash and that Earth does not have the components to easily build new ones. Flower of the Pond is an engineer and could make them, but it would take her years."

"Unfortunately while trying to convert me to her cause, she mentioned that she was already pregnant." Sheila's face looked embarrassed as Mind Ripper explained his error. "In my defense when we mated she swore she was using birth control as is required by our people's space exploration crews."

Sheila took over again. As she talked she flipped the projector's control and pictures of the space craft, the zombies, and the destroyed bridges flashed on the screen. "Mind Lords can lay up to three hundred eggs at a time. They can breed once every three months by our time scale and the young can breed for the first time within four days of hatching. They were designed to be infiltrators and weapons after all. It took a very short time to conquer their creators and our projections hold out little hope for us should they get off the island." She took a deep breath. "So aside from an alien with advanced technology breeding a hive of body snatching children and working like hell to contact more of its kind to come join in with, presumably, a lot of very nasty alien weapons we also have zombies running around with no explanation." She took a deep breath. "Which is why I have gathered all of you here. Since you do not know one another I will make introductions."

She moved to the chair immediately to her left. The woman in it was pleasantly plumb and curvy. Just under four and a half feet tall with a mix of Chinese and African features. Her skin was a pale gray color, as if she had not seen sunlight in years and judging by the fangs peeking over her bottom lip, she had not. Her curly black hair was very long and in dozens of small braids that hung down to her waist and were studded with rainbows of beads that clattered when she moved. She wore a skintight white leather outfit that covered her from neck to ankle, matching platform shoes, and held a dominatrix style leather mask in one hand that presumably went with the rest that included a bag-like thing on the back to hold and cover her hair.

"Forgive the look," she said in a hillbilly-like accent. "I like to avoid sunlight."

"Queenie here is a vampire. She was a prostitute in eighteen hundreds Spain, the daughter of a Chinese hooker and a black railroad worker. She was attacked by a vampire and came awake three days later in an alleyway where her body was left to rot with no idea what was happening to her."

"I did a little trial and error for a while," the vampire said. "Got into a bit of trouble here and there for a few years. Then I saw a play about a new book called Dracula. Practically a how to book."

"Unfortunately for her it was also a how to book on disposing of vampires."

Queenie nodded. "That it were. At the time I'd been running a brothel of my own full of vampires, thinking safety in numbers was a good thing. Someone had gone and destroyed the bastard who killed me about a month after I was turned, making make a master vampire... head of the line with a few extra powers... but when the heat started to turn up on my little business I decided to uh... pull up stakes and go to America. I figured a whole parcel of coffins being shipped off would attract attention, so I done killed the whole lot of the undead whores I had workin' for me and headed out on my own. Settled out in Appalachian country among the hillbillies where they barely ever heard of reading let alone Dracula and where a man might disappear into the woods any old time. Got myself a strip club... called 'em bordellos back then... and settled in nice and cozy like."

Sheila nodded and moved to the next chain. The woman in it was a good-looking Mexican woman wrapped in a fur coat. She had golden-brown hair down to her shoulders, thick black eyebrows, a Mayan nose, and luminous green eyes that briefly flashed yellow. "Real name unknown, but you go by Luna. I've been looking into eye witness accounts and you seem to have shown up in places where a lot of truckers have gone missing."

"What witnesses?"

"Nobody saw you kill anyone, but well... let's just say you're pretty distinctive."

She sighed. "Oh, you mean these..." She opened her coat for everyone to see. There was a lot of staring and even an appreciative whistle. Beautiful enough but not striking, it was still no wonder people remembered her. Under her clothes she wore nothing and her breasts had been clearly visible. All three pairs. They were in descending size from D to C to B-cups. Each with large... nipples was the wrong word so Sheila went with teats. These were definitely not human looking, though she doubted anyone would care. What skin they could see was spotted like a leopard, only with pentacles of various sizes. Like tattoos only the color looked too... natural somehow. Just darker shades of skin instead of ink. They dotted her from the neck down.

"I can't prove it, but you're some kind of werewolf, right? The animal attacks that follow every place you go are a bit of a give away. And from what I can tell you must be something special because I've found references to you going back to the sixties."

Luna smirked up at her. "Nice detective work Sherlock." She spoke English but with a slight accent that made her E sounds longer. When she said it the word sounded more like 'dee-teck-teeve'. "Yeah, I'm a werewolf. The baddest werewolf ever. You see back in the early sixties while other girls were off being hippies I ran away from home and was paying my way by working as an escort. Me and a bunch of the other girls got called out to a party in the desert." She snorted. "Turned out some bastard had a party in mind alright and we were the snacks.

"I was locked in a cage with dozens of other people. Men, women, and children. Our captors were teasing us. I could not hear much but they were talking about hunting us. That it would bring them all together. From what I've pieced together someone wanted to gather all the different werewolves in the country into some kind of army. Skin walkers, cursed werewolves of all kinds, lycanthropes, people possessed by wolf spirits… to tell the truth I still do not have the slightest idea how many kinds there are or were." She leaned back in her chair and put her bare feet up on the table. "At the time I thought they're just crazies until the sun sets and they all start to change. That's when all hell broke loose.

"I don't know exactly what happened. I got trampled by the other captives when they saw the monsters and panicked. Broke some things and knocked me out cold. They eventually opened the cages and of course everyone ran screaming, trying to make it into the desert. Which was what the wolves wanted. I came to and saw them chasing people down left and right. I was still lying in the cage so they ignored me and I got a good view. It was a nightmare." Nobody seemed inclined towards sympathy so she went on. "So there I am lying there, certain I am going to die. I decide, what the heck, I'll take myself out the easy way and maybe get a bunch of them too. I crawled out and went to their cars. They weren't locked and I found a siphon and I'm not too bad at doing a blowjob. Soon I had the whole area doused in gas.

"The pack came back, a raging sea of bloody monsters. Don't know if they were drunk on their own power or just stupid, but they all ran at me as one. The last human left, helpless and bleeding. I sat there, not moving. I think… just before I flicked the lighter… they realized what was happening. But it was too late and we all went up just as they dog piled on me."

"And then?" Sheila prompted.

"I woke up in the desert," she said. "Covered in these damned stars and with extra boobs so I knew something was off. I was confused and felt strange. I got up and looked around, but the cars were all trashed so I walked to the nearest road and hitch hiked to get a ride. Got picked up by a trucker who got a little fresh and I was feeling… emotional." She smirked. "It was quite terrible what I turned into. And even worse what I did to him." She shrugged. "It took me a while, but I found a groove. I need to eat a lot of meat, especially when I change and unfortunately humans are often the only thing around that fit the bill." She looked at Sheila who showed no reaction. "One day I managed to talk with a shaman in Arizona. He told me that when you kill a werewolf you sometimes take on their curse. All those different kinds, all that magic hitting me at pretty much the same time, did some weird things to me even by monster standards. I'm not like any werewolf anyone's seen before and I've learned to enjoy it over the years. Been shot with silver and it hurt, but did not kill me. It's possible I can't die." She shrugged. "Not that I've tested it." She looked at the person next to her. "So who is the midget?"

"I am not a midget!" Rang out a high pitched voice with an English accent.

Sheila moved to the next chair. It had three phone books stacked on it and the tiny woman did look like a midget, except she was perfectly proportioned. She was bald, not a hair anywhere on her body, even eyebrows. She wore a sensible black dress and comfortable children's dress shoes. She was almost flat chested with nice toned legs and arms. Her golden-brown skin and hooked nose with a gold ring in it were definitely distinctive and gave her a sort of Arabian Knights feel. She wore two rings on each finger, gold and ornate with large gems, several earrings, and had other piercings that were less visible. There were a couple of large bolts through her nipples that Sheila could make out under her top and she was sure something under her skirt had made metallic clinking sounds when she moved.

"Officially you are listed at Norma Tut." She looked at the woman. "Your past is mostly fake IDs and I've managed to trace you back to the early nineteen hundreds. More specifically to a small Egyptian tomb that was discovered in eighteen seventy and placed on display in nineteen ten. Interestingly someone switched out the mummy with another dried up corpse and the original was never found." She raised an eyebrow. "Coincidentally at the same time one of the assistants on the dig went missing."

"Okay I admit it, I'm a mummy," she said. "Nafertut, former priestess to the gods of the land of the Nile at your service. Call me Tut, for short."

26

Someone snorted. She glanced at Luna. "For the record, everyone was this small thousands of years ago. It's not my fault people today are all giants and have different standards of beauty." They all stared at her. "Hey, it's a touchy subject. I don't know which is more annoying, the teasing or being hit on by closet pedophiles all the time."

"How did you end up a mummy?" Sheila asked.

Tut smiled and said, "Let's just say I'm the reason they started using eunuchs to guard priestesses and harems. I mean, come on! We spent two thirds of the year cooped up together in skimpy outfits. They expected me to keep that stupid vow of chastity?" She shrugged. "Someone blabbed to the priests and the gods were not too amused either. I was cursed to walk the earth for all eternity and buried alive." She smirked. "Until some tomb robbers found me. You call them Egyptologists, but the curse on my tomb did not really care. You open it and you're a tomb robber."

"Which brings us to exhibit D," Sheila said.

The girl in the next chair looked like she should be either in college or a hospital. Her hair was an unnatural shade of blood red that seemed to move on its own. Her skin from stop to bottom was cut with deep marks in strange patters. They were deep cuts that seemed to go all the way to the bone.

Except no matter how you looked inside was just darkness. She was also wearing a large pair of sunglasses.

"Carla Thomas, whose file aside from the hair matches you exactly, disappeared in regards to a murder case fifteen years ago. It seems that a sorority on campus had been involved in what was listed as a 'Satanic Cult'. All of them were found dead in what looked to investigators as a ritual gone horribly wrong. Some were killed quickly and cleanly while a few seemed to have been torn apart. Carla Thomas went missing, but considering how much of her blood was found at the scene nobody believes she could have survived."

"It's amazing what some humans are willing to deal with to try to become rich and famous. Call me Silk." The girl lowered her sunglasses. Where her eyes should have been were rough gouged out sockets. Inside was darkness, completely black except for the occasional twinkle of what might have been distant stars. Never the less you had the feeling of something slithering around in the dark. Even the other monsters shuddered.

"It turns out those girls were great at summoning things from the beyond. Not so good with binding spells to keep what they summoned in check. Carla was lured to their sorority in exchange for promises of popularity and a place on the cheerleading team, only to be sacrificed so the cult could become rich and powerful. She was dying in excruciating pain when I showed up, drawn by the ritual. I am not particularly fond of mortals trying to use me for their own benefit so instead of making a deal with the cult I offered her revenge in exchange for her body."

She opened her mouth and something lightning fast and dark as night that could have been a sucker or a tentacle shot out and took a few of the chocolate ants from the bowl on the table, bringing them back to her mouth Just past the human teeth red fangs pressed forward, rows of them. They snapped shut on the treat with an ugly scraping sound. In her eye sockets a glowing orange eye with a goat-like pupil peeked out of one hole and then the other before she slipped the glasses back on and for the world looked like a human girl again. She giggled and it had echoes that sounded disturbingly like a group of children laughing in the distance.

"What are you exactly?"

"A being from beyond this plane of existence where the very laws of nature are different. You call us elder gods these days, since Lovecraft got famous. Think of this body like a video game avatar and I'm at home using the controls. It's actually more like a hand puppet, but most people today do not know what that means." She looked over at Tut. "The kind of gods you worship created this world and in such a way that my kind cannot actually exist here. We consider that a little unfair."

The mummy girl shrugged. "I'm none too happy with them myself."

Ignoring the byplay Sheila moved on, giving Silk a wide berth. "Finally we have our celebrity, Mary Patches. You may know her by another name: Frankenstein's monster."

The final woman was nearly nine feet tall not counting her hair, which added another foot, and had a special chair. The others had been ignoring the way that even sitting down she towered over them. She wore a white lab coat that did nothing to hide her breasts straining against the front. They were enormous even for her size and strained against the top of her coat. She was beautiful in an inhuman way. A little too perfect, like a CGI character. Her hair was white and stuck up like an anime character, a black line down either side. Stuck in it were various and obviously used pens and pencils. Her skin was a dozen different shades from nearly black to pale white, in odd geometric shapes. A patchwork quilt only with no stitch marks. In her eyes the irises came in several different colors and the pupils glowed LED blue.

"My ex-boyfriend was really into body building and making friends."

"Not exactly Herman Munster are you?" Silk said.

"I took my first name from Mary Shelley's, but my origins bare no resemblance to her fictional story, though it was based on what really happened." Her voice was a seductive purr. She looked at Sheila. "How much do you know?"

"I got my hands on the lab reports and Dr. Cane's computer files."

She smiled, showing off large teeth that were bigger than human, but looked normal in her mouth. "Then by all means, feel free to tell my story for me."

Sheila nodded. "It seems that there really was a mad scientist at Castle Frankenstein. An alchemist anyway. But his efforts were not directed towards restoring life like in the book, but prolonging it. Dippel Frankenstein even invented a special oil that was used for a variety of purposes… and possibly dynamite years before Nobel managed it. His greatest experiments were relegated to myth and legend and revolved around the search for immortality. He created something. A creature that escaped into the nearby woods and for years was the subject of local legends.

"Skip ahead to the nineteen nineties. Dr. Michael Cane was on vacation in the area and after his tour of the castle went for a walk in the woods where by chance he found the creature… barely held together after a hundred years of living feral in the forest."

"My brain was the success," Mary put in. "It is indestructible and the brain stem and even spinal chord can regenerate. Sadly it was damaged in the process and I was more animal than man. The rest of me... was not in much better condition. Alone in the woods for a hundred years I was falling to pieces."

"When he came upon you the good doctor realized what you were and took custody of you, smuggling you back to America in secret. I don't know the details but he found funding among some of the less savory areas of the government and soon had a research lab under a small college where he could experiment. He claimed he was building them a super soldier."

Cupping her gigantic rack the huge woman smiled with perfect lips. "I'm afraid Michael had something different in mind."

"He also did not use random dead bodies like his fictional counterpart. No, that would never do for his creation. He was obsessed. He used the most advanced technologies. Experimental nanites. Cybernetic components. Things you would need twelve PhDs to pronounce let alone understand. And most disturbingly, at the same time girls from the local college began to disappear." Sheila and the others noted the patches of different colors on Mary's body. "The FBI was sent to investigate the case. A case which was later declared solved when a cult on campus was found dead."

Mary glanced at Silk. "Huh, small world."

"You have *no* idea," Silk told her ominously.

Ignoring this Sheila said, "The bodies were found when his project came up for review and the government sent people to check on his progress. Most of them were preserved in the lab's large freezer, along with the mangled body of Dr. Michael Cane. The 'super soldier' was never recovered and eventually declared to have never existed, the fever dream of a madman. The whole thing was abandoned and literally buried. Care to fill in the blanks?"

"Oh no problem," Mary said. "You see Michael was really into his project. First for the science but eventually for the companionship. He wanted to make me perfect. The perfect woman. Beautiful with the best parts. Intelligent. Completely insatiable in the sack." She licked her lips and arched her back, a button on her coat popping off revealing some more of her cleavage. She puckered her perfect lips in a brief kiss. "I think he succeeded."

"You turned on him?"

"No, of course not. My brain was augmented with information, wi-fi, and his programming. Not Isamov's three laws… that would not exactly work with his super soldier plans when he recreated me… but I couldn't turn on him if I wanted to." She sighed wistfully. "No, I'm afraid dear Michael merely forgot certain aspects of cause and effect when he made me his perfect woman. You see as soon as I was perfected to his satisfaction and off the slab… well he wanted to get right down to it and I was only too happy to comply with reckless abandon. I know it's a bit slutty having sex one minute after I was born, but that's how he made me. Just out of the box and raring to go so to speak with very few moral inhibitions and no restraint."

"What does that mean?" Luna asked.

Sheila said, "According to the autopsy Dr. Cane's body was *severely* damaged. They compared it to a case involving a mafia snitch who had been run through a junk yard car crusher."

Absently Mary reached over to one of the other empty chairs. It, like the others, had been bolted to the plane's floor. This did not matter as she daintily picked it up with one hand and lifted. The bolts snapped free without effort and she held the chair in her hands, gently crushing the solid steel frame like it was an aluminum can.

"Have you ever seen the pulp collector in a juicer after you've run a lot of fruit through it?" Mary asked with what sounded like real regret. "Poor Michael. It was my first time you see. I scratched and bucked, and clenched… until he ran through my limbs like putty."

"Ouch," Queenie said. "I know that one."

"Ditto," Luna said. "I guess monster virginity is going to be a bit messy to lose."

"My first time just turned to dust when I sucked his life force and fluids from his body," Tut said.

Silk held up her hands. "Don't look at me. My beauty is literally skin deep. Anything goes deeper than that and it is not coming back. I don't have any human internal organs even so sex has no appeal for me. My enjoyments in this universe are more cerebral."

"I've seen your DVD rental accounts," Sheila said.

"Aren't you going to tell them about yourself?" Mind Ripper asked.

Sheila hissed, "Shut up!" Suddenly she had the whole room's attention. She sighed. "Fine. I'm not exactly human either."

"You smell human," Luna said. "I can hear your heart beat."

She glanced at Queenie who looked at the ceiling with fake innocence. "Well you see when I was sixteen I was... dealing with some things. I lived in a small town and my parents found out I was gay. So they immediately signed me up for psychiatrist appointments and forbade me to ever date. I knew it would never work, but for two years they insisted.

"My older brother Ted on the other hand, was more supportive and helped me sneak around and when I turned eighteen he decided to give me a special birthday surprise. He got me a fake ID and told my parents we were going to a concert a few towns over. And instead he took me to a strip club."

"My strip club," Queenie clarified.

Sheila took her own seat and grabbed a hand full of chocolate covered ants, shoving them into her mouth and chewing while she gathered her thoughts. "It was great at first. I was so excited and then…. I caught sight of this woman." She looked at Queenie. "Our eyes met and it was like a dream. We stared for a moment and then she seemed to just float towards me. We didn't say anything and then we just… kissed."

The vampire looked down, wrapping her arms around herself. Her sharp nails dug into her arms. Blood welled out and then was sucked back in. She glanced at the others. Luna looked disgusted. Mary and Tut were both smirking though Mary looked more predatory. Silk just looked bored. "I don't know why I did it. I just… couldn't help myself. I even bit my own cheek in surprise."

"Oh I see," Tut said. "And she got a taste of your blood while you were kissing, making her a thrall."

"A thrall?" Mary and Queenie asked.

"A blood slave," Tut explained. "Master vampires are called the kings of the undead because like necromancers they can turn other people into undead. Ghouls, werewolves, weaker vampires, and a few others. Sometimes it happens just by being near a person, or do it on purpose when they bite someone... those kind of curses work like radiation and can infect people. The more powerful the magic involved the more likely. I don't know about you but I could probably turn someone into a mummy if I wanted and Luna here could bite or scratch someone and turn him or her, but vampires... they have all kinds of tricks. Probably because the first ones did it to themselves on purpose instead of being cursed.

"Something else they can do is giving a human a drop of their blood. Makes them stronger, basically eternally young, and the vampire's loyal slave. They not only obey but practically worship the vampire who turns them. Later they might be turned into a more powerful undead, but their basic purpose is to act as guards in daylight hours when the vampire is weak. They don't have the vampire's weaknesses and would literally die for their master."

"It wasn't on purpose," Queenie protested. "I didn't realize what I was doing. I've never made a... thrall before. Just vampires. I mean... I had never felt that way about a girl... or anyone really. I was emotional and confused. I am an undead monster and from a time when two women... well it simply wasn't done! Never even crossed my mind. Then suddenly there I am… gah!" She covered her face.

"Meanwhile I finally open my eyes and behind Queenie a couple of her employees, two other vampire strippers, are tearing my brother apart." She shuddered. "I tried to help, but she held me back and there was nothing I could do."

"I realized what I had done, though I never knew the details. I know about Renfield in the book after all. I felt and saw her reaction to her brother and it hurt me as much as her. I realized I was feeling her emotions. So I told her to leave and not come back," Queenie said. "To live her life as if she were a normal girl and never come back until the end of the world. She turned and ran from the place. I never saw her again."

"Her first order to a blood slave and it freed her… that had to be rough," Tut said nodding. "Not to mention sending away your love at first sight like that."

"It hurt." Sheila said. "For both of us. I went home. Told my parents what happened and called the police. They all went up there… then came back all glassy eyed and told me everything was fine."

Luna snorted. "Look deep into my eyes huh?" Queenie shrugged. "So then what?"

"Eventually I left town. I didn't know what Queenie had done to me but before high school ended I knew I was stronger… healed quicker… didn't feel pain as much. Had the urge to eat insects and small rodents. I saw Dracula so I knew I was basically Renfield. The urge to go back to Queenie was there and strong, but she had ordered me not to. I decided to put my new gifts to use and join law enforcement. Ended up in the FBI working drug busts, usually as bait. I worked my way up the ladder. Over the years everyone called me 'Baby Face' because I always look so young and yet I could still kick the ass of even the strongest biggest men in the bureau. I never went back home. And then I got sent to investigate a UFO crash and suddenly I had an alien attached to my spine."

"It's not easy," Mind Ripper said. "Her body constantly heals fast and rejects me so I have to readjust my grip. The others were killed though, so I was out of options."

"So that's how you escaped Zombie Island when the rest of your crew was killed," Silk muttered.

"Correct. I went to Queenie for help," Sheila said. "It was the end of the world after all."

Mary nodded. "I see. But where do we come in?"

"Normal means aren't working and what the alien is doing is going to come to fruition soon. Satellite tracking shows the zombies herding large groups of surviving humans together. Lots of them… more than even her babies could take over." She shrugged. "As if that was not enough."

"So you have a zombie army and you want us to fight it? Why should we?" Luna asked.

"For the same reason I picked all of you."

"You want to sleep with us?" Tut asked. "Because you're gay and I'm noticing a distinct lack of men in this group."

"I used to be one," Mary pointed out, seductively crossing her legs. "And my brain is still technically male. Not my fault I never got the chance to use that portion of my anatomy."

"I often feel like I'm trapped in a woman's body," Silk added cheerfully.

"No," Sheila said, ignoring this. "I mean sure you are all pretty and I find myself still wildly attracted to Queenie here. Judging by the nude paintings of me in the back room of her club she feels the same about me…" The mortified vampire covered her eyes with a hand. "But no. I picked all of you for two reasons. One is you were the best I could find." She shook her head. "I only have jurisdiction in the US and the pickings were slim. I found a boy band of male mermaids, but they can't be out of the water for more than five hours. There was an elf working at Santa's village swapping out children for changelings, but he's from fairyland so I couldn't trust him helping me and I had him shot. There were a handful of others, very few of them very useful for this.

"The rest of my potential recruits are all important well connected men and women who I could not get close to without warrants and even then they would have had an army of lawyers at their side. Only four people in this country including Queenie *might* be master vampires and since the weaker ones combust in sunlight, they're basically useless for this. I've tracked people who could be sorcerers, vampires, psychics, and god knows what else. Do you know how hard it is to prove the existence of a mind reader or someone with magic powers when they do not want you to?"

"Yes," the women chorused happily.

"You five were on the short list of powerful and useful monsters that I could actually get my hands on."

"So what is the second reason?" Mary asked.

Sheila looked around at them. "You're all bimbos." They looked up at her. "That is not meant as an insult. Look, with the exception of Mary here, you're not the sharpest fangs in the vampire's mouth. Since I knew magic and monsters existed I took it more seriously than most, but I found you all fairly easily." She pointed at Queenie, "You aren't exactly low profile and I knew where you were already. You have the local authorities pretty sewn up, but when I got a hold of the police report on my brother's case it said 'The boy simply decided to leave town and promised to contact his parents later and *I will forget I was told to write this*'." Queenie winced. Sheila looked at Luna. "You add to your income by working for strip clubs and robbing truckers I assume you kill as you travel the country and people remember a woman shaking six tits in their face either on stage or while hitch hiking. I tracked some of their stolen credit cards in similar cases going back decades. Even when you are careful every four months or so you leave a string of missing truckers and abandoned trucks in your wake."

"I go into heat, okay?" Luna snapped. "I get turned on like an animal and… shit happens." The other monsters nodded in understanding.

"I don't care," Sheila said. "It's not like I'm trying to haul you in, even if I could get my bosses to try putting this shit in the system." She looked at Silk. "You starred in porno movies entitled 'Sorority Sister Sex Cult' one through seven, which starts out with the words 'Based on a true story'. You've also been living in a mansion where you have a cult of followers who pay for everything you want including taxes and treat you as a…"

"A goddess," she said. "Seriously you humans will worship anything so why not take advantage? As long as I don't try to start a public religion or tell people about other planes of existence the other gods leave me be."

"It's not exactly low profile." Sheila eyed Tut.

The mummy sighed. "I got lazy, didn't I?"

"You're working in the Egyptology department at a university and are considered one of the leading experts in the field. For anyone else that would be impressive as hell. For you... yeah, pretty damn lazy. Also you go out at night and do midget mud and gelatin wrestling for spare cash. I hear you're in the championship round next month."

"You people these days are so damned tall... and a girl has needs. Money, sex, and to devour the occasional life force to keep from turning back into human jerky. When a big biker guy with a record goes missing at places like that... the police don't exactly look too hard. Especially if you aren't tall enough to ride a roller coaster. It used to be easier to hide before they put cameras everywhere."

"I'm just glad I don't show up on camera," Queenie said. "Kind of a pain when I go in to get my license renewed though."

"How did you find me?" Mary asked. "I stay in my secret lab and focus on experimenting with mad science. I know I've been well hidden even if I do sometimes need human test subjects. I have an Internet connection in my brain and check constantly for any mention of myself."

"You have a tracking device in your abdomen. It was in your schematics. The point is," Sheila said as Mary stared down at her own belly, poking her rock hard ten-pack of abs with one long finger. "You were all easier to find than the average monster. You all are sluts and more importantly killers who feed on humans to prolong your own unholy existences, to get you things, you want, or for twisted experiments. And you are not that good at low profile because you like spending money and showing off your boobs. All of you have worked as strippers for cash at one time or another and even hookers even though as monsters you never really needed to. Hey, I'm not judging. I worked as a hostess at one of those clubs myself to pay for college."

Queenie laughed. "Everybody is a 'hostess' and nobody strips." They all laughed, even Sheila.

"Aside from that, most of you need humans to survive because you feed off of them or need them for other things. You all like the world the way it is. You're self centered and superficial. I thought that would be a way to get you all to agree for your own benefit if not that of the human race."

"I do love daytime TV," Silk admitted. "And Bonbons." Something tongue-like flickered over her lips wetting them with something like saliva. A drop landed on the table and hissed sending up a puff of green smoke.

"I live the American dream of a business that is 90% profit and all my employees are my slaves who I pay in blood, a dark building to live in, and daytime Internet access," Queenie said. "The world is definitely better to live in now if you are a vampire than it was a hundred years ago, especially the night life."

Luna put in, "I personally don't want to go live in the woods if I can avoid it. I'd miss the simple things like fur coats and toilet paper."

"Hey no need to sell me," Tut said. "When I was alive we didn't even have toilet paper. Though we did have something to wipe our asses and do our work for us instead of machines." She looked at Sheila and smiled nastily. "You are Jewish, right?"

"Right and Moses kicked your people's asses." Sheila looked at all of them. "So how do you think your lives are going to be if the world ends? If humans are all either zombies or the hosts for alien parasites? No more TV, advanced technology hunting you all because farmers hate when predators pick off the sheep, and slowly starving to death because humans are bagged and tagged or turned into zombies. Maybe not right away, but give it a century and see where you stand. Like I said, you're all bimbos. You like the simple life, the finer things, being rich or at least comfortably well off, and not having to do much for it. Most of what you get you do with your powers and sexuality.

"You're all vicious monsters who probably belong dead, as the saying goes, but you're also powerful and you have a vested interest in humanity's survival. So here are your choices. You can either help me save the damned world, or you can continue to sit on your... admittedly attractive... backsides hoping someone else will step up until the whole thing collapses around your ears."

Sheila waited while the others shared looks. She knew Queenie was in already. They had talked long into the night and both had regretted not being together for years. Sheila missed her brother, but the initial attraction she had felt to the vampire was still there and the urge to serve her that came with being her thrall had all but washed away her fears and doubts. She still missed her brother and hated that he was killed, but she could not deny how she felt and Queenie had admitted that she felt the same way, as much as it still freaked her out even after ten years apart. Now that they had the chance to reunite neither wanted to waste it.

Finally Luna threw her hands up and said, "Fine. I'll do it. I'm stuck here for eternity and I definitely prefer amusement parks and fast food to shambling zombies. I'm in."

Mary smiled. "It seems like a definite chance to learn new things and like she said, I have to live here. So why not?"

They all looked at Silk who sighed and pulled out a cell phone. She hit a button and after a moment said, "Hey Greg, it's your lord and master. I've got to avert an apocalypse so could you guys record all my shows and make sure you stock up on my favorite snacks? Yeah if I fail you will all have a place in my kingdom and so on... Yeah. Yeah. Right. Hail me. Later." She hung up. "Schmucks. Okay I suppose I'm in. What the hell, you only get summoned from the outer realms once every celestial epoch."

"I'll take that as a yes," Sheila said. "Thanks to Queenie and her hypnotic powers of persuasion I have unlimited backing from my superiors and a substantial raise. Tell me what you think we'll need and I'll have it waiting for us when the plane lands."

Headquarters

FBI HQ was near the edge of the sea with a view of the closest point of the island. There were military patrols as far as the eye could see and gun placements every few feet. It had taken them thirty minutes, even with clearance, to get past the blockades. In the distance there was the occasional crack as the snipers and surveillance posts got an ID on a zombie near the shore and took the chance to shoot it. The shield over the island did not stop lead. It was more, Mind Ripper said, designed to repel iron ore meteors and the like. In the water were dozens of ships and in the air circling helicopters kept an eye out for anything slipping in and out.

When they arrived, delivered in a large army-green SUV with Mary riding on the back since she would not fit inside. As they got out an older man in a suit came forward, removing his sunglasses. "Agent Casey."

"Director James," Sheila replied. She wore a similar suit and removed her own sunglasses.

He glanced at the other women getting out of the camouflaged vehicle and frowned. Queenie was wearing her full body white leather dominatrix outfit that kept her skin completely covered but was so tight it might have been painted on. She could go in direct sunlight she had assured them, but it sapped her strength and made her uncomfortable so she covered as much as possible. She even had a pair of welding goggles over her eyes and the mouth was zipped shut. No holes even for her nose. Luna was wearing her fur coat, wrapping it around her as she swept forward, a look of distain on her face as she eyed the soldiers. As someone who was at the top of the food chain for the last few decades Sheila's training in profiling told her that she had grown to consider humans in general second class citizens, only a step above cows because they were more dangerous.

Silk had chosen to dress in a Lolita style black dress lined with white baby doll lace. She even had on fishnet stockings and carried a black lace umbrella. Her hair was done up in two long pigtails on either side of her head. She walked across the gravelly ground towards them in stiletto heals. Meanwhile Mary got off the truck, which groaned in seeming relief as her weight was removed and it rode higher on its shocks. She was dressed in a new lab coat with thigh high black rubber boots laced up the side and matching fingerless gloves laced up to her elbows. She had put her hair into a bun.

On the ground she helped Tut out of the SUV. The tiny woman was dressed in her teacher outfit that she used for work, a sensible dress and a pair of cat's-eye glasses on a chain that Sheila knew were fake. Sensible shoes and what had to be a padded bra. Sheila suspected that being around the other women and their large breasts was hitting her a little in her ego, especially since by ancient Egyptian standards she had been a beauty. Then again by today's standards the real Queen Cleopatra had been pretty damned ugly. Tut was pretty enough if a little flat chested and child-like due to her size. Next to Mary she looked like a ventriloquist dummy.

"These are your handpicked team?" He asked.

She nodded. "We are clearly dealing with the supernatural here even if the scientists brought in refuse to admit that sir. Or the paranormal at the very least. These are the best experts I was able to find."

"What about those people down in New Orleans you were looking into? The priests and the psychics?"

"Too difficult to determine if they are real or fakes sir," she said. "We don't have time to test them all and can't trust them to keep their mouths shut if we let them in on this. I needed definitively supernatural experts and these five are the best I can do without serious backing."

He nodded. "Understood. What intel can you give me on this?"

"None." He glared at her. "These women have their own lives sir, existing outside the law. They prey on humans. To ensure their help I have to develop trust with them and ensure they have reason to help us. They are basically immortal and unless destroyed will still be here when we are all dust. I'm appealing to their self-interest. If we try to track or contain them then they may just let humanity burn or do it themselves. After all if we go out they are doomed anyway and I would not like to see what they do when backed into a corner."

Hr gritted his teeth. "I don't like this plan of yours."

"I don't expect you to sir. I'm compromised in ways you can't even begin to comprehend. But this is a doomsday scenario and right now we're all in it together. If Osama himself came back from the dead and showed up right now and offered a platoon of suicide bombers I'd accept their help."

He nodded. "Agreed. God this is insane but… fine. We'll deal with the Devil. I've already signed off on it. If you pull this off we're freaking heroes and I guess letting a few… whatever the hell they are… run free for a while longer is a small price to pay. If it goes bad we're all dead anyway."

Sheila nodded. "Did you get the supplies I requested?"

"Truck loads just incase other teams need it later. Though I have to admit, after losing those task forces this was hardly the kind of request I was expecting."

"Welcome to the weird side sir." She looked at the others who were listening and not caring to hide it. "What do you want to do first?"

"I'd like to get a look at one of the zombies," Tut said. "Something about what you've told us is bothering me. Do you have any captive?"

"Yes, we've retrieved a few. But even those we recovered in tact dropped dead once we removed them from the island," James said. "That was one of the deciding factors when we tried to blow it up the first time."

"Not surprising," Tut said. "I'd still like to see them." She looked at Silk. "Want to give me your insights oh great and omniscient deity?"

"Sure," she said.

"I'll want to hear what you find out about them," Mary said. She looked at James and said, "Give me all the data you have on the situation and I'll need access to a chemistry lab… I'll give you a list of what I need. Ferrous metals don't make it through the shield?"

James frowned, not liking being talked to as if he were a grunt, but he needed them and he knew it. He had worked with special and even black ops before. Why should they show him respect? "Correct."

"Will you be able to make it through or should we leave you here?" Sheila asked.

"I'd prefer to go with the group," Mary said. "I'm sure they have men here who may not be as smart or capable as I am, but will do an adequate job as can be from here. I'm more ceramic than metallic internally and most of the rest is heavily shielded. Michael wanted me to be able to pass metal detectors. If I can't get through I'll return and do what I can here."

"I think we'll just take a look at what weapons we can find and maybe get lunch," Luna said and jerked her thumb at Queenie. "After all we're here for our physical skills, not our brains right?" Queenie nodded.

"Sounds like a plan," Sheila said. "I'll liaise and coordinate things while we're preparing to go in."

James frowned. "You know the other agencies are not just going to step aside."

"Hey, more power to them," Sheila said. "If they can solve this thing then we can all go home and pretend it never happened. Maybe it'll be like in the movies and there's some super secret government monster squad or something that handles things like this."

"What makes you think there isn't?"

"From what I've seen sir, monsters don't play well with others and our government can barely keep the NSA in line, let alone creatures that have been alive longer than this country has existed. I won't say we don't have any in the government for whatever reason, but considering the lid we're keeping on this if they exist by the time the truth works its way up the line to anybody powerful enough to do anything, it may already be too late."

His shoulders sagged. "I hope you're wrong Sheila. I really hope you are wrong."

An hour later Sheila found herself observing more than anything and began checking in with the others. Luna and Queenie were off to the side. Luna had a pile of wrappers nearby from a local rob place. She had put away more meat than her small frame should have been able to handle and now she was lying in the sun. Queenie was sipping from a straw stuck in a thermos; her lips unzipped enough to let it in. Sheila could feel the vampire watching her silently and could not deny the thrill she felt at her interest. She had dated a few times over the years and knew that Queenie was basically responsible for her brother's horrific death, but no matter what she had done the initial connection they had felt for each other had never faded.

When she had gone in to talk to Queenie and bring her in on this, the vampire had brought her to a back room where there were dozens of paintings. Paintings of Sheila. Of Sheila nude. Of Sheila with Queenie. It was very flattering and erotic and the vampire definitely was a good artist with some interesting kinks that, if they survived this, Sheila would like to explore. It did not help that this close they could sort of sense each other's emotions, like what some people said about twins. Sheila did not like to admit it, but she knew that if Queenie asked her for anything be it a potato chip to self-immolation she would do it without question, happy to obey her mistress as a dog when the owner is holding a treat. It was almost a need to obey her like the need to breathe. Likewise she also got a thrill by the way Queenie refused to order her around despite that and kept sending her an embarrassed mix of shame and lust like a teenage virgin at prom with a guy she has already decided to sleep with that night.

Damn it was complicated. If the world ended it was probably because of whatever the two of them had. Which, admittedly combined with Queenie being the ultimate bad girl, made it even more tempting and romantic.

"Ditto," a voice purred in her head and she was awash with Queenie's feelings again, making her shiver.

"Are you alright? Your body is doing… odd things. Pumping hormones and…" Mind Ripper said.

"Never mind," she muttered and turned her head away from the two monsters, reclaiming control of her vocal chords. "I can't wait until this is over. My head is getting far too crowded." She was doing her best to act like an emotionless FBI agent. The last thing she needed was spending the rest of her career hearing Mulder and Scully jokes because of this. She was dealing with a bunch of weird shit including her own emotions for a woman who qualified her as a necrophiliac on top of everything else. She had an unstoppable hunger for insects and rodents that she managed to keep in check in public, but all the stress was making her hungry and she was eating bags of chocolate covered grasshoppers from her personal stash like popcorn to take the edge off.

Much more of this crap though and I'll be stress eating sand crabs, she thought to herself. She was already fighting the urge to dig the wiggling things out of the beach.

Moving on she went to where the other three were pouring over computer files, print outs, and three dead bodies. They were pretty professional about it, if you ignored Mary's constant flirting. She was obviously collecting and easily understanding the data, but she kept flirting with the men and women around her and had even disappeared for fifteen minutes with some of them to god knew where to do god knew what. Since then Sheila and the others had kept an eye on her, making sure she stayed on point. It was not easy. Several soldiers had come by, drawn by rumor, to stare and occasionally try to show off for the mysterious group of women. Sheila had them all sent away quickly, but there were a lot and they just kept coming and Mary was no help. She was designed to be the ultimate sex toy, so what could you expect?

Sheila just wished she could explain that these men were dangling meat in front of the tigers and that any of her hand picked team was likely to give in to temptation and they might start disappearing. Since there was nothing to do about that, she moved forward and asked, "What do we know?"

"Nothing good. I've hacked some satellites to scan the island," Mary said. "I have plenty to work with. Aside from the US tasking everything they've got the other countries that have any have so many hovering over the area that they're close to causing a traffic jam. Not all of them know what's going on, but they are interested." She showed Sheila a laptop. "Infra red is working best for determining the pockets of zombies and humans. I guess since the aliens are cold blooded they do not think about that. I'm looking at the energy waves of the shield. Near as I can tell it's centered in a small town near the center of the island, away from the major cities."

"Can't you get a better view from traffic cams, ATMs, or cell phones?" Sheila knew hacking like this was illegal, but who cared?

"Nope. A lot of the power grids are off, either intentionally destroyed or failing because there's nobody there to maintain the equipment and contact with anything actually on the island is cut off." She pointed around. "Looks like there are a lot of small groups of people bunkering down and keeping to zombie hordes at bay."

"Who doesn't know how to handle a zombie apocalypse these days?" Sheila asked. "There are books at the library on it, a thousand movies, TV shows... Hell the CDC had a web page."

"Right. Well the zombies are still attacking them, but some are escaping and swimming for it. The Coast Guard collects them and puts them into quarantine to keep it from spreading incase they are bitten and also to keep them from blabbing. The rest are, as far as anyone can tell, going all *Walking Dead* and doing their best to shoot as many zombies as possible.

"Meanwhile the zombies are doing their best to turn every human they can and many are walking patrols to keep an eye out for intruders. I've found some spots where we can enter the island unseen. Meanwhile most weapons are going to have to be left behind here and we'll have to scavenge some once we get past the shield... which I have to say is impressive." She smiled beatifically. "I'd love to get a look at the machinery that can do this."

Sheila looked at her. "You said on the plane that you've been interested in mad science. What do you mean by that?"

"I'm the result of experimental science, given a computerized brain and a body that comes straight out of science fiction. My original creator was an alchemist, not just a scientist." Mary looked into her eyes. "I can access the Internet with my brain and access any human scientific knowledge so no point in that.

"Then there are things like our... associates over there." She nodded towards the other undead women. "They defy nearly everything humanity knows. Yet they exist. If my brain were completely computerized the thing would have probably exploded just from meeting them and there are… places online dedicated to such things. So that logical part of me insists that I find a scientific set of rules to explain it all… which gives me something to do to kill my time.

 "In addition, most of the world's great inventors were not focused on science, but the occult. Leonardo da Vinci wanted to create flying machines when such things were considered impossible. Galileo investigated the idea that the world was round and was killed for it as heresy. Tesla found alternating current, but when he died he was also working on a death ray. Most of the communication devices we use today were originally designed to allow people to contact the dead." She shrugged. "So I have dedicated my time to exploring… fringe science."

 "Such as?" The people sent to retrieve her had been repelled by strange weapons when they tried to enter her lab and since that was not the objective they had to leave it.

 She grinned and said, "I think I'll keep a few secrets. If things go wrong on the island, as they almost certainly will, then I'll demonstrate. Until them I'll keep my discoveries to myself thank you. I am not particularly comfortable with humanity getting their hands on anything like me, let alone some of the things I know."

Sheila could not argue with that. So she left Mary to her work and went to where Silk and Tut were standing next to some guys in HAZMAT suits and examining the bodies of the zombies. The doctors and scientists had been unhappy letting them near the bodies without them, but the girls had refused explaining that they were immune to the disease and despite their fears since the zombies had crossed both salt and running water they were probably neutralized. Only a few undead could handle the sea and most of them had trouble being on land for more than a day every few years.

"Learn anything useful?"

"Yes," Silk said. "But it's all bad news."

"Do you see any marks on these bodies?" Tut asked. "Besides the obvious bite marks and other damage?"

"Uh… that one has a tattoo of a mermaid on her arm and that guy has a bolt through his cock. Aside from that… nothing much."

"Exactly," she said. "To get a dead body to move you have to curse it and that is done one of two ways. With me it was a direct curse from priests and a god… so no marks. Same for master vampires and their victims who are connected through the master. The other way is through symbols. Writing.

Usually attached directly to the body, which is a pretty involved process. Our werewolf friend has both kinds on her… but you've seen the pentagrams. Look at Silk here."

Silk stretched and posed, showing off the odd cuts on her arms. "As part of the summoning ritual they carved these into the former owner's skin and channeled me into it. That's why I can inhabit this body. It was prepped."

"A curse like this can be spread by contact," Tut said. "Depending on how powerful the original is. A bite, blood transfer, sex… these make it more likely. Dark magic is sort of like radiation that way."

"Trust me, you do not want me hanging around a cemetery," Silk said. "Not unless you want the residents getting rowdy."

"Werewolf bites pass the curse right away because they aren't actually dead so the magic connects more easily. Killing a werewolf on the other hand can pass the curse too as part of the link between killer and victim. Killing a lot of monsters… and the chances go up. A vampire who does not intentionally turn someone, their victim might come back if they want to live enough. Or their body might rise without their soul as a revenant… a type of vampire that is a lot like a zombie. They usually fry at the first sunrise because they are not smart enough to hide unless a master vampire controls them, but most do not bother. Necromancers can turn you into just about any kind of undead with the right spells and ingredients."

"So what is the problem?"

"These zombies aren't possessed," Silk said. "You can slap a spirit, god, ghost, or demon into an empty vessel like these with proper preparation. But these are soulless zombies with no will of their own."

"Usually that kind of undead walks around randomly acting on animal instinct, usually hunger," Tut said. "There's a reason the world hasn't been overrun like this before. They aren't smart enough to pose much of a threat and zombies without a supernatural being holding them together usually rot and fall apart after a few days if not actively killed. The further down the line of undead you go the weaker they are. After about three generations from the master vampires can't even make more vampires, which is why masters usually do not make many either or they might turn on them for power.

"You have to cast other spells to keep the zombies together and there are costs for that sort of thing, both physical and spiritual. Vampires have to drink blood to keep moving and they have a vulnerability for every power. Like they can hypnotize people so garlic repels them. They can fly so they can't cross running water. That sort of thing. Where as werewolves only self heal and transform, so they only have real problems with a few herbs, fire, and silver."

She looked over at Mary. "These things been running nonstop for the better part of the month and easily passing the curse on to nearly all of their victims. 70% of the human population of the island are pretty much zombies at this point."

"So they're getting power from somewhere?"

"Yes. Either they have a god or demon helping them…"

"Which doesn't happen much these days," Silk said. "For the last few hundred years immortals have taken a low profile because mortals got all creepy about it. Like rock star fans."

"Or more likely the reason the zombies have been collecting all the extra humans together and whoever is running them is sacrificing those people to use their life force to power the zombies."

"Which means that once they run out of people, the zombies drop," Sheila said. "I mean I'm saddened by the loss of life, but it's good to know that they're trapped and won't be spreading across the world like in the movies."

"Agreed," Silk said. "Now if there were not a body snatching alien with advanced technology who wants to bring her people to Earth involved we might be in the clear."

"And if they did not have far more humans than they need gathered for that," Tut added. "From the look of things they could keep the zombies up and moving for weeks to go before they run out and that's way longer than Mind Ripper suggests they need."

Mary came over, "From what I can tell they are centered around one town where the force shield originates and being kept in a mall. We can't see much through the satellites, but the heat signature says there are thousands of people being held there and a lot are still being brought over by the zombies. Which Tut assures us is overkill."

"Even I only need to suck the life force of one person every three or four months to keep my girlish looks," Tut said. "Vampires need maybe one victim a month unless they exert themselves too much. Werewolves are alive and their bodies go through massive biological changes so they need to eat a lot of meat, but not magic. Sucking it out through a ritual or with magic is more effective, like the difference between sucking the juice from an orange or using a juicer and while there are a lot of zombies, they're not being kept in pristine condition so maybe three or four a day would be more than enough."

"So what? They're keeping the extras on hand as backup?"

"Or for something else," Silk said.

Tut nodded. "Necromancers doing something this big usually have other plans than a short lived zombie army. Where do you think vampires came from? Someone wanted immortality and power and they were willing to pay the price."

Sheila frowned. "Then why doesn't this happen more often?"

"For the same reasons we're helping you," Silk said. "Who wants to live in a world full of rotting corpses? Even necromancers need normal people, if for nothing else but to lord over. Most of them end up working in finance, summoning the dead for inside information, eliminating their competition, and the like. Once you've used your powers to make yourself immortal, rich, and powerful in this world generally you sit back and enjoy it."

"Why immortal? I mean once you know there's an afterlife…"

"Oh some get bored and let themselves die eventually," Tut said. "Believe you me, my people were obsessed with this stuff. The thing is when messing with dark forces you can either end up cursed so you can't leave this realm of existence until the end of time…" She gestured to herself. "Or you make a lot of enemies on the other side who would don't mind waiting forever to get what passes for their hands on you."

"We eternals can be very vindictive," Silk assured her, smiling cutely.

Sheila nodded. "So where do they learn this crap? I know there are a lot of books on magic, but I can't imagine it happens too often."

Silk shrugged. "You're right. When people do know this stuff they usually keep it to themselves. No need to piss of the angry villagers or risk having competition."

"There was a major sorcery war in London last century in Europe," Tut said. "Magicians like to use or eliminate other power wielders. Another reason monsters tend to stay in hiding." She looked at Sheila. "You should know about that. King Solomon enslaved all kinds of things to his will."

"Then you've got psychics who use their extra senses to see through time or just know things. Amateurs who play at summoning spirits and said spirits, having nothing better to do, clueing them in." She snickered and Sheila remembered those cultists who had summoned Silk in the first place. Suddenly she had a suspicion on who had clued them in on how to do that and why their binding spells misfired. One of them had owned a Ouija board. Sheila remembered a comic strip she saw once where a man was shooting at a werewolf who did not seem to care and just happened to be wearing the same tie as the guy who sold him the "silver" bullets he was using.

"Sometimes you get taught by family or just find old books and cursed amulets, or something gets written down in a fantasy story that they try and it works… basically your dark arts starter kit."

"If it works they become rich and powerful and have no reason to rock the boat," Sheila said in understanding.

"Then you get Flower of the Pond who is suddenly giving them access to other worlds," Mind Ripper put in.

"It's a risk," Tut said. "But according to you, the alien can't read minds and she's only been here a month and the zombie thing started right away. Too soon for her to be behind that part of this."

"So they have to be working together."

"Not a bad deduction for a bunch of bimbos, huh?" Silk teased.

Sheila nodded agreement. "I never said you were stupid."

Tut said, "But that leads to another *major* problem."

"Which is?"

"The zombies are organized. Millions of them all at the same time. They're walking patrols. Dragging off living people without killing them. Not wandering blindly into the sea."

"But there's nothing inside," Silk said. "These bodies aren't prepared to host anything and I checked. Nothing intelligent has set up shop in them. Nothing that should be able to think like that."

"Which means…?"

"You ever play a video game?" Silk asked. "Imagine trying to control one character for every zombie on this island. A human can't do that. Necromancers have driven themselves mad trying to control a fraction of this number. Maybe up to a dozen if they are really intelligent and kept the instructions very simple. I could do it. Your friend Mary here might. Some random teenager? Not a chance. Her head would explode."

"This is why a lot of necromancers form cults. More people working on it means more zombie minions. Plenty of replacements if the over extend themselves or the magic backfires." Tut smirked. "I was a priestess after all. But that's what you need priests for. We don't just control the dark stuff; we use white magic to purify the people and places involved so evil undead don't rise and turn on everyone. Dark wizards don't usually bother and it builds up like toxic waste. It gets too bad and the gods might step in and wipe them out."

"We don't like it when people break our toys," Silk said.

Mary had been listening and absorbing this information. "So what you're saying is, that there has to be a large group involved. But I haven't seen any evidence of the numbers you would need for that wandering around the place. The zombies are unsupervised and most of the living people are stationary, not wandering too far from their bases or near the zombies."

"I said a human can't do it," Tut said. "From what Mind Ripper said, the alien can't be helping with this either. She's mortal."

"Which means whoever it is has other help. I'm pretty sure it's not from the Other Side. As near as I can tell while the gods are, as always, watching I'm the only one directly involved in this clusterfuck." The way Silk said it made it clear that no other higher powers intended to get involved either.

"So what is it?"

"My guess is she's created a... I'm not sure what the word is," Tut said frowning. "It's sort of a super zombie."

"A wight? Spelled w-i-g-h-t?" Mary suggested. They all looked at her. "I've been looking things up online while you talked."

"A good enough word. It's a human cursed and enslaved by dark magic. They get hideously twisted by the forces involved and are forced to serve the necromancer. Not like Sheila here, more like when vampires hypnotize people and take over their will. They do not want to serve, but have no choice." Tut went over to where a dry erase board was set up. "The wight is used like a leader." She drew a stick figure. Then two more below him then below that a few more until it formed a pyramid shape. "The wight can drain life force like any undead but those it drains become zombies. There's a connection that lets him control it. Simple orders unless the wight is real focused. It can see through their eyes and other senses. The zombies do what it wants and he can send them energy by feeding on the life force of others."

"So you're saying the necromancer uses the wight to control the zombies and all they have to do is control the wight," Sheila said. "If we find and kill the wight, what happens?"

"The zombies would be released and act like normal zombies until they rot like normal in a few days," Tut said.

"Great," Sheila said. "I mean it sucks for the wight, but..." She stopped. "Can you work up a picture of what this guy will look like? We can make him a prime target. Take him out."

"Good plan," Tut said. "Zombies on their own tend to only attack humans. Without a controlling mind they would probably ignore us since we're not. We could walk through them like they are not there. Decapitation and burning the body to ash will kill it, just like a ghoul."

"That would be helpful," Mary said. "Except that it and its master are probably in the center of all the other zombies... who I doubt will just sit there and let us barbeque their bosses." She tapped the computer screen. "With the human food source and the alien technology. And maybe alien infested people too by the time we get there."

"The eggs should be laid by now.... I'm not one hundred percent on how you measure time on this planet, but they will hatch soon and will be influenced by their mother when they hatch. Our minds take time to develop and that was never an intention when we were designed. It took centuries for us to really evolve into a society."

"Probably less time than us," Sheila said.

"But that's the point," Mary said. "Why is the necromancer helping something that hijacked her body? From what you say showing off like this will attract a lot of attention from other sorcerers." She looked at Sheila. "Captain, you said that the girl she merged with was a teenager?"

"As near as I can tell."

"And you're having trouble controlling Sheila who is just a thrall... so whoever this is has to be working with them to do the zombie thing and human enough that the alien can stay merged with her... which I'm assuming they would since otherwise they could not trust each other like this. So probably human and she really is that age instead of just looking like it like us. I mean we could all pass for anywhere between seventeen and twenty, but if the movies are right anyone that can regenerate like that would not be a good host."

"The old normal bullets popping out of the werewolf thing," Silk said. "Right. Like Wolverine."

"So the question is, what is this girl getting out of the deal?" Mary asked. "We've established that on Earth she could use her powers to get wealth, power, and everything else. The way she is going about it she's exposing herself, getting involved with alien body snatchers, and basically endangering it all."

"She could get off of this planet," Mind Ripper said.

"For what? I know you seem to breathe okay here, but I doubt your people even have food we'd like. The same for clothes, money, and anything else."

"Mine wouldn't," he said. "I can live here because I am implanted with nanites that help me to survive. So is she and they are passed on to children. On our world a normal human would die instantly. So no, we don't have much to offer." He paused. "But your people might."

"Ha," Mary said. "Look, I am a secret government experiment. Believe me, our people aren't going to trade for alien tech. There's a reason she's hiding on this island. If our people caught sight of her they would put a bullet in her head and take the ship and the alien engineer. Especially after all this. She's a clear and present threat to the security of this country. If she were lucky they'd lock her to a bunker under the desert and extract everything she knows about necromancy and alien technology."

"No, not the humans on this planet. The ones out there."

Everyone stared. Sheila would have too, except the words had come out of her own mouth. "What?"

"Humans have been in space for decades. You work interstellar security, have contacts, colonies… as I understand it they take maybe half a million specially chosen people off the planet every year and do their best to keep anyone else away without special dispensation."

"Really?" Mary pursed her lips. "Makes sense. Wouldn't want terrorists or something getting off the planet. And why bother telling us?"

"Plus it would interfere with your wealth," the alien added.

"What wealth?" Tut asked.

"In space most things aren't worth anything. We have matter replicators. Food, clothes, machines, and anything else can be made cheaply. So the only thing worth anything is cerebral. New information, inventions, and things.

Human society is based around entertainment. Your games, movies, television, books, and the like."

"That's why I'm still on this planet," Silk confirmed.

"The humans out there do their best to keep bootleggers off the planet. They trade rights to come here and examine your species to the grays for scientific information. Some planets have banned anything from this planet for the adverse psychological effects. It's complicated, but to keep up the flow they don't want to let the ones they leave on Earth know about it or they might change everything."

"So there are people out there…" Mary said, sharing a look with the others. "And they probably don't believe in magic and monsters. I mean if it were widely known then Mind Ripper would not be surprised. If they have them out there we've established that the supernatural keeps a low profile or risks destruction."

"So a teenage girl with magic powers that she normally can't use suddenly has the chance to travel the universe… in exchange for our planet," Sheila said.

"Flower of the Pond would easily promise such," Mind Ripper said. "Especially if she could deliver such powers to her people. It can be taught?"

"Oh yeah," Silk said. "Believe me, this sort of thing isn't limited to Earth."

They all sat contemplating the possibilities. Around them the sounds of the military echoed. Finally Tut asked, "So what do we do about it?"

"We kill them," Sheila said. They all looked at her. "We get to the island, get to the source, and we kill them all. Mind Ripper, do you have any problem with us wiping out Flower of the Pond's kids? They're yours too."

"They were never supposed to exist. My people live on other planets. Legally we aren't supposed to be here and I am opposed to everything Flower of the Pond's group stands for. Our original hosts were incurably war-like and subjugated long ago, but infesting another world like parasites is wrong. The sooner we eliminate the possibility, the better."

"Well alrighty then," Silk said. "Genocide it is. We work our way to the source, pop the necromancer and anyone helping her, smash some alien bugs, and maybe loot a few stores on the way back out of town."

"You really think it'll be that easy?" Tut asked.

"Maybe not, but we're all basically immortal. How bad could it be?"

Sheila looked at Mary. "Will you do the honors?"

"Gladly." She reached over and gave Silk a meaty slap on the head.

It did not hurt her, but it did surprise her. "What was that for?"

"Sheila is right, you are a bimbo. You'd think a god would know about a jinx."

"Oh." She paused. "Sorry."

Sheila shook it off. "Okay. Get what equipment we can carry onto the island. We'll have to salvage anything made out of metal once we're there so that won't be much. Mary print everybody off maps of the island and where we're going incase we get separated. Tut can you make up any spells or something that will protect us?"

"No," she said. "Most of them would work on us too. There are a few things we can take that seriously inconvenience zombies personally, but…"

"Okay. Anything else?"

"We're going to have to take a boat… no engine… to get in. That's how the Special Forces guys they sent in did it after the shield went up. Otherwise the shield will rip the engine right off while we're still out at sea," Mary said.

"That's a problem. Most undead don't do good around running water and salt. Messes with certain magical forces. Vampires and mummies are definitely on the list."

"Like the headless horseman," Mary said.

"Trade offs," Sheila said. "Which means what?"

"Which means that close to the ocean Queenie and I will be essentially dead bodies, unable to move, until we hit land again."

"I might have trouble controlling my body too," Silk admitted.

"Also if we lose Mary to the shield and Sheila, we'll be stuck there until we can find someone else to move us off. Luna should not be affected, but she's something weird as far as werewolves go so who knows? And I'm including when we go on to the island and if we leave." Tut looked at Silk. "Which means we will be vulnerable. If we manage to turn off the shield then the government will probably blow Long Island to Hell immediately."

"She's right," Sheila said. "They've had thermite missiles trained on the island for weeks, waiting for the slightest flinch. That stuff burns hotter than the sun."

"Will they aim for that many civilians?" Tut asked.

"Yes," Mary said. "Officially there's already an outbreak that's killed seventy going on eighty percent of the populace and New York is right next door. Maybe half of the higher ups have a clue what's really going on and at least a dozen other people who can authorize the missile strike think it is a plague and none of them will risk whatever caused this hitting land."

"So how was Flower of the Pond planning to escape?"

"I'm sure she's thought of something," Mind Ripper said. "She's not stupid."

"That much fire power won't kill me, but my body will be reduced to ash," Silk said. "I'll be banished back to my own universe."

"I'll be left bodiless too, a wandering spirit trapped on this planet," Tut said.

"My brain might survive it," Mary said, "Everything else won't. That much heat can vaporize anything. If I survive it I'll be back in a jar in some government lab somewhere…"

"It's more than enough to finish off me, Queenie, and Luna," Sheila said. "But we've already established that if we don't do this then life on this planet won't be worth spit anyway, so what's your point? We won't destroy the shield except as a last resort. We'll burn that bridge when we come to it. Anything else?" Nobody had anything. "Fine, I'll get Queenie and Luna up to date and we'll set out in half an hour."

Infiltration

The rowboat cut through the water at remarkable speed. Half of its passengers were useless. Tut, Silk, and Queenie were secured together and attached to the boat with chords. The mummy and vampire were dead to the world. It worried Sheila even though she had been warned this would happen. Silk was still mobile, but she moved slowly like a drunk and could not speak properly. Mary had to sit very still in the middle of the boat, which had extra inflatable pontoons attached to the sides to keep it from sinking under her weight along with their backpacks. Leaving Sheila and Luna to row.

"At least we don't have to do this in New Jersey," Mary commented as they rose and fell over the waves.

"Jersey isn't that bad," Luna said.

"No, I was just thinking how much worse this would suck if we had to deal with the Jersey Devil on top of everything else."

Sheila laughed. "Yeah, because we really need another monster thrown into the mix."

The boat struck bottom. They managed one final push then the three of them got out and pulled it onto the shore. When they were out past the damp sand suddenly all three of the others snapped awake.

"How do you people shower?" Mary asked.

Tut said, "It takes a lot more water... like a river... to mess with us. We can even use pools, though it does weaken us. Just do not expect trips to the beach or the water park."

Queenie unzipped her lips and smirked. "Of course back in the day we didn't have to shower. Just wash down in a pan with a bit of water."

"In my day we didn't even do that," Tut added. "We just slathered on layers of scented oils and then scraped it off when it got too thick."

Luna shook her head. "Yuck."

They unloaded the boat and checked their gear. Each of them carried two ceramic knives. Some sticks of dynamite... sadly with fuses instead of detonators and a box of matches. Changes of clothes, mostly skimpy things so there was plenty of room. Queenie had some spare blood packets.

Without power most of the blood banks were probably useless and there were not too many people or animals available either.

Luna had a lot of jerky. Mary had some vials of strange things she had concocted at HQ and a few she had brought from home, but since Sheila had no idea what they did she did not bother listing them as supplies. She was wearing a solid black outfit with various pockets scavenged from the military, but the other girls were used to being invulnerable and preferred to stick with the skimpy clothes that "both distract and make it easy to move". Truthfully Sheila thought they just liked dressing like sluts, but knew better than to say it. Even Luna had left her fur coat back on the mainland and switched to a pair of cut off jeans and a tank top. She was really well muscled. Not as buff as Mary but still built. It was all Sheila could do not to make a *Twilight* joke. Tut was tiny and skinny with tiny almost non-existent boobs and a slightly bigger butt. Sheila and Silk were both thin but attractive teenager types and Queenie was plump and curvaceous and the only one still wearing the same outfit as before. Sheila just hoped vampires did not sweat.

"You're sure there aren't going to be any zombie animals?" Luna asked for the twelfth time. "Because I don't need zombie rats crawling over me." She shuddered at the thought. Apparently being a bloodthirsty immortal monster did not rid you of childhood fears.

82

Tut said in an exasperated tone, "I told you, the control spell relies on the law of similarity like Voodoo dolls. They could make undead animals, but the human zombies can't because they are not the right shape. Undead animals haven't been seen by any of the surveillance and if they did make them you couldn't give them orders because the animal-wight could not understand the commands. So what would be the point?"

"We'll keep out eyes open," Sheila said. "But we're all immune to the bite right? Even me?"

"I think so," Tut said.

Queenie put an arm around her. "You're all mine."

Blushing Sheila forced down a smile while the others rolled their eyes. "Okay then. Until we're attacked by zombie bears or a thousand undead rats, we'll assume the animals aren't an issue." She pointed to Mary. "Can you still access the satellites?"

"Nope," she said. "My connection shut off when we got past the shield. I memorized the maps though."

"And we all have copies," she said, patting a pocket. "So our first objective is to get some transportation. It's a long way to our destination and I don't want to walk it. Who here can hotwire a car?" She raised her hand. Everyone else did too. "Great. Let's get several. Luna, you have the best sense of smell. You and I are going to go look for gas."

"Okay, but the pumps probably aren't going to be working."

"Hey, you told me you know how to siphon a gas tank, didn't you?"

The werewolf laughed. "Good point."

"Silk you hold down the fort. Meet back here in an hour."

They split up, all watching the woods. Once Sheila was out of sight Queenie said, "Hey, can I... ask you two something?"

"What?" Mary asked.

"Well like I said I've never been with a girl before... have you?"

"Once or twice," she said. "I'm usually too busy for long term relationships though. I only do it because I'm programmed to. Michael was a bit kinky and wanted some girl on girl action."

"I used to," Tut admitted. "Back when I was alive. We spent most of our time alone together in a harem and weren't supposed to touch the men. And there were some pretty erotic rituals we had to perform together. We didn't really consider it sex so much as... helping a sister out. Relieving some stress. We did not even know you could do most of what they do today back then, you know?"

"I know," Queenie said. "I was raised by hookers in Spain in the eighteen hundreds. When you're a prostitute you don't even kiss and foreplay... forget about it." She licked her lips. "I mean I barely ever even... enjoyed myself. It was just a job you know and it got old fast with the men. If you had suggested before then that I be with a woman I wouldn't have known what to say. Sure a few come to my club but...me? I never thought it would happen. Now I've spent a decade obsessed with this girl and here she is again. The zombies and aliens are a twist, I'll admit..."

"But Sheila's different from any girl you've met before?" Mary said, looking around for enemies. Most of the zombies had been pulled back since the sea damaged them, but a few were on patrol around the edge of the island for when people tried to get in and out. So far they had not seen any. Also there were not many cars. After things got hairy most people either went home or headed across the bridges before it was cut off, so there were not a lot around the beach at the moment.

"Yeah," Queenie admitted. "I mean I never kissed a girl before. When I did... it felt like when I feed only different. I felt my legs go weak and everything in me seemed to tighten up and if I had to breathe I wouldn't have been able to."

"Yeah, well the main effect of an orgasm isn't between your legs," Mary said. "It's actually a blood rush."

"Look we've all been around for a while and it's obvious you like the girl. You just have to get over the school-girl phase and get on with it," Tut told her. She winked at Queenie and said, "Or not. I mean it's only the end of the world. So you may be running out of time. Or we win and you can spend the next hundred years or so getting up the courage to kiss the girl. Whichever." She suddenly looked up. "Jackpot!"

The other two watched and saw that their little friend had spotted a dune buggy next to the lifeguard station. She rushed forward and found the keys already in it. It took a little stacking of some life vests on the seat, but she soon was behind the wheel and revving the engine.

It took a little while but eventually they found a restaurant a ways down the road. The windows were broken in and there was a lot of dried blood and even a dead body missing a head. Presumably a zombie. Outside there were half a dozen cars. Queenie picked a police car. Inside she found a shotgun and a quick check of the restaurant turned up two dead police officers, the keys, and the cop's pistols. Queenie eyed the dried blood. "What a waste."

"I don't think I can fit in any of these," Mary admitted. "No trucks or SUVs here… I usually ride a special motorcycle I built myself."

"There's a convertible," Queenie said. She looked at her own car and an idea struck. "You ever see *Police Academy?*"

They went up to a classic red convertible and Mary decided to hotwire it rather than go back and search through the bodies for the keys. It took her three seconds. Once it was running they ran the engine and lowered the top. She could not fit in the front seat, but they ripped those out and tossed them aside. Sitting in the back seat she fit okay and got the car moving as they drove back the way they came. The only problem was that under her weight the car tilted to the left a bit.

Waiting for them Luna and Sheila each carried two large red plastic gas cans full to the brim. Luna was also chewing on some mints she had acquired somewhere. Queenie pulled up next to them and lowered the window, looking at Sheila. "Need a lift?"

"Thought you'd never ask." She opened the back, tossing in the gas before slipping into the front seat. The other cars had no room for them anyway. Luna looked between the two cars and Silk immediately hopped in next to Mary. So she went over to the dune buggy.

"Move over short stuff," she told Tut.

For a moment she considered arguing, but she could barely see over the dashboard and the life jackets were uncomfortable so she scooted over so

Luna could drive. Queenie took the lead while Sheila began fiddling with the guns. Being FBI trained she knew how to handle them and that was immediately apparent to everyone, so nobody argued.

They pulled off only the nearby highway just as a group of zombies came shambling around the corner. They moved pretty fast actually, in a jerky kind of way, but it was too late and the cars easily out paced them. Sheila was tempted to shoot them, but knew that it would just be a waste of ammo.

"So," Queenie said. "You, me, and a drive in the country. Not bad for a first date."

Sheila smiled and reached over to squeeze her hand through the cool white leather glove she was wearing. "Your hand is a little cold." A human's would have been warm, but still it was not unpleasant.

"You'll just have to warm me up then," Queenie said, biting her lower lip, her fangs dimpling it in a way that reminded Sheila of a kitten. She squeezed harder and leaned so that she could lay her head on Queenie's shoulder.

Suddenly a horn honked and they both jumped. They looked over their shoulders and saw Luna and Tut behind them, laughing. Presumably behind them Mary and Silk were too. Queenie growled, a sound like an angry tiger, and rolled down her window. Reaching out she extended her middle finger.

They honked again and if anything laughed harder. And for a while the unlikely convoy rolled on.

It was too good to last though. They had barely gone half an hour before they had to stop. Someone had piled a bunch of cars in the road. A few and they could have pushed them aside and moved on, but they were about thirty deep and buried the road in a rainbow of hoods. It looked like their engines had all been torn out after they were parked, parts strewn across the road.

"What the hell is this shit?" Luna asked as they got out to investigate.

Mary nodded. "A good idea. I'd guess the zombies did this."

"Why?"

"To block the roads so people could not drive," Sheila said. "They can't keep up or drive so they force people to go through town and avoid the highways. Probably have the same thing in all the cities. They've had time and more than enough manpower to do it."

"It's not like they need the sleep," Tut agreed.

"So we do have to walk?" Silk asked. "Isn't there an airport?"

"A plane wouldn't get high enough to work before the shield got it," Mary pointed out.

Queenie said, "I could fly, if it were night."

"Fat lot of good that does us," Luna snarled.

Sheila considered. "Better not. We should stay together as long as possible. Let's take a look in that town we passed at the last off ramp. Maybe it's just the highway."

It wasn't and soon it became evident that it was easier to walk than try driving around in circles. So they reluctantly abandoned their cars and began hoofing it. All of them moved faster than a human would have, especially in the kind of shoes they wore, but even superhuman abilities could only move them so fast. Queenie even ended up carrying Sheila who was not nearly up to their speed. Sheila was a little embarrassed about that, but for the vampire it was like she was made of feathers and she barely noticed the weight.

Sixty miles per hour in heels should have gotten them through town fast enough, but they kept running into problems. There were indeed a lot of cars stacked in the major roads and it was not long before they found their first group of zombies. Only a couple dozen, but blocking their way and while not as fast, more than enough to delay them.

"Damn it," Sheila jumped down and lifted the revolver. Seconds later with inhuman precision she put a bullet into the brain of fifteen oncoming undead before the gun clicked empty. She had the ammo, but it was in a box so she holstered it and swung the shotgun around, taking out another six.

"Nice shootin' Tex," Queenie said. "But save the bullets."

"Yeah, you brought us along for this, right?" Luna growled. She had sprouted fangs and claws. Her eyes glowed yellow and a thin covering of her grew over her skin like velvet. Other than that she still looked human.

"That's what you turn into?" Tut asked. "I was expecting something a little more… impressive."

Luna laughed. "Trust me munchkin, when I really transform you'll know it." She and Queenie waded forward.

Sheila was unsure about this and so were Mary and Tut who took up fighting stances. These things had taken out dozens of special forces groups sent in to deal with this situation, most of them armed to the teeth. Mentally she knew that Luna and Queenie were supposed to be powerful monsters, but despite a few differences they both looked like relatively petite young women. Every bone of her that had trained as an FBI agent told her she needed to step up and go first.

That feeling faded quickly and she was left with her jaw hanging open. Queenie and Luna waded into the zombies that reached them first and clawed at them. Their movements reminded her of girly-girls in a slap fight, scratching at one another. Nothing like the real marital arts stuff she had been taught at the FBI or even what you learned in a woman's self defense class. But where the unstopping horde would have easily overwhelmed an armed human being the girls shrugged off the clutching hands like they were children. Luna's claws did not scratch like fingernails, but sliced through flesh and bone like they were passing through air. Blood and pus sprayed up and would have covered her, but by the time it fell she was already gone, dismembering the next zombie. The stumps where their limbs an heads used to be looked as if they had been sliced off with razors instead of an animal's claws.

Queenie presumably could have done the same, but she was more delicate. She reached out and it seemed like she was plucking flower petals instead of rending the zombies limb from limb. Heads came off in her fingers as she gripped and lifted. Tendons tore and bones cracked, but so easily to her that they might as well have been affixed with papier-mâché. The zombies' bodies were still moving and twitching, the brains still in tact, but without their arms and legs they could not move and their mouths opened and closed silently as if chewing on the air.

"Impressive," Mary said. One of the walking corpses managed to slip through and she lashed out, slamming a fist into its chest. The rib cage imploded, practically turning inside out. Had she been completely human Sheila would never have seen it. As it was only Mary's government manufactured sensors saw inside the body where its bones turned to shrapnel, shredding its insides like it had stepped on a land mine. The zombie was launched through the air like a cannonball into some of its fellows and then crashed into a nearby wall, spraying congealing fluids over it like paint.

Silk extended one hand and from the cut in her palm a black tendril flashed out like a whip at a trio of zombies. Then it retracted and the zombies moved forward... only to fall into dozens of small pieces. She raised a blood red eyebrow and said, "If you say so."

Soon the whole group of them were lying in pieces. Queenie and Luna returned, not so much as a drop of fluids on their clothes. Queenie bowed dramatically and motioned to a side alley not littered with body parts. "This way ladies."

Miles away in the Southward Mall a girl sat on a golden throne. Truthfully it was the chair they used at Christmas when Santa's village was set up and kids lined the mall to ask for presents. But it was gold and had a soft cushion and without the candy canes and elves it looked quite impressive.

The girl in it was Bethany Jones. Japanese, the daughter of immigrants who had moved to Long Island before she was born. Her hair was dyed ice blue and she wore black leather clothes she had looted from Hot Topic. Her nails were painted black and her eyes had turned complete inhumanly dark weeks before.

Around the mall the shops were closed, their steal gates lowered. In each one was stuffed dozens of people who sat around. They were being fed with food from the mall and local stores brought in by the zombies, but they had all given up rattling their cages long ago. Neither the girl nor her monsters cared and if she got annoyed sometimes she would stop feeding them. Or more likely take notice and use them for the next round of sacrifices. It was amazing how seeing her use a knife to rip the still beating heart from a man like some sort of Mayan priest while the zombies held them down suddenly made everyone feel like being quiet and not attracting attention.

Then there was Brock. He had been a handsome boy. Quarterback of the football team with a scholarship in his future. He had not known Bethany had existed until their senior year of school when she had come in suddenly transformed from the two hundred pound pimpled geek she had been to the prettiest girl in school. Even then Brock had a girlfriend he cared about, but something had come over him. One day all that mattered was Bethany.

Now he knew why. The evil witch had cast a love spell on him. A spell that had been broken and replaced by his current situation. He had known nothing about magic, but in the months he had been enslaved to her will if he learned nothing else about Beth, it was that she liked to talk. And gloat. Especially about her powers and plans. And her serial killer actions. While they had been building up the zombie army she had cackled gleefully about what it was like to run her hands through someone's entrails while they were still alive.

She had started out playing with an Ouija board. She had contacted a ghost of another witch, a man from the sixteen hundreds named Jebidiah. He had taught her things, summoning spells mostly, in an obvious attempt to get her to allow him to possess her body. Bethany had played along but when she had milked him for all he was worth she had instead banished him to the afterlife the old ghost had been trying to avoid.

Then she had begun summoning other things. Learning from each and then betraying them one after another. Her power grew until she practically owned the whole town. Her parents gave her everything, spending her college funds and their savings on her. When that ran out other people mysteriously started giving her things. She made herself beautiful. Soon the whole town was under her spell and she had plans. Oh yes, so many plans to carefully spread her power.

Then the alien had come. It had taken over others first, but it could not fight the compulsion that controlled its new bodies. It realized who was really in charge and it came for Bethany. Yet she resisted as well, her dark power fighting the strange creature for control until they reached an impasse and they began to talk.

Flower of the Pond admitted to her plans to take over the Earth for her people. Bethany admitted to hers. It turned out that they did not conflict much, although the girl was a bit put out by the alien body-snatching thing. Until the alien told her of the worlds beyond Earth. Where there were people waiting with amazing technology and no concept of magic. No defense against the things Bethany could do and no other sorcerers waiting in the wings to retaliate.

All she had to do was help the alien engineer. It would take time, but they could gather what they needed to contact the alien's people and call for another space ship. Earth did not have that much technology, but she could build it with time and resources. In the mean time they could get those by allowing her young to infest a few billion humans and grow into an army. Bethany had countered with an army of her own… temporary true, but effective if done right. Able to keep anyone from finding Flower of the Pond's young until they were ready.

So she had summoned Brock and worked new more hideous enchantments on him, twisting his form and enslaving his body. His mind was freed in the process, but he could no more disobey her or act against her now than he had before. Inside he could hate. He could realize what she had done to him… to everything… but he could not do anything about it. God he hated her.

Standing next to her throne he caught another glimpse of himself in the shiny metal surfaces of the mall. No hair, his eyes and skin were solid white. He had long teeth like a crocodile that stuck out of his mouth because they were too big to fit. He could open it wider now, enough to bite a human's head off. Not that he needed to. His touch could paralyze them and suck the life from their bodies. He only needed to bite those Bethany made him turn into zombies. His hands were large and stretched out, ending in six inch white claws. Ditto on his toes. His nose was long and pointed and his ears stuck out, elf-like from his egg-like head.

Brock was hideous now.

He would have given anything to get his claws around Bethany's throat. To tear her head off in a spray of blood. Lord knew he had been forced to do it to other people enough by now to be certain he could. But he was bound by her will and she had ordered him not to even say anything bad about her.

"Mistress, there is a problem."

"What is it?" She asked.

He looked at her. "Some of my zombies were destroyed. Quite quickly in fact. A few minutes later another batch perished and I feel a third dying as we speak. When I look through their eyes I see a handful of... really hot women, but that is all before the zombies are destroyed."

"Are they prettier than me?" She teased.

"Of course not," he lied. True Beth was gorgeous as only someone who had chosen how to look could be, but to Brock she might as well have been made of snot. Too bad he could not actually tell her that. True she might destroy him or at least torture him, but that would have been a relief.

Her voice changed as the alien spoke. "Send more zombies until they die just like with the others."

He did not have to obey the alien, but saw no point in fighting it. Bethany always backed up its orders if he balked. Mentally he sent out the command feeling like a murderer. Even more because the last few groups he had intentionally killed with his own slaves had been burly Seal Team people and the new ones were sexy women. Sure the zombies had killed hundreds of similar girls, but randomly and not because he specifically condemned them to die. Still he had no choice and with what Bethany had planned, whoever they were, they were better off dead.

The plan had evolved a bit since the girl and the alien had begun to explore what they could really do together. The alien was a religious zealot. Bethany was a narcissistic teenager with access to dark powers. Their plan was to skip the planet and they had unleashed a zombie horde that had already killed everyone they knew. Why not go all out?

So Bethany had mentioned a spell she had learned but could never perform before. It required time. It required a lot of power and preparation. And it required a large number of human lives as a sacrifice. Considering what the result would be if it worked, and so far all her spells worked, that was almost incidental to the carnage that would await not only Earth, but also every other world for all eternity. Worst of all he would probably have to stand next to Bethany through it all, listening to her rant and giggle every step of the way.

Brock envied the women as hundreds more zombies began to close in around them.

Absently he stared at the fountain in the middle of the mall. It had been shut off, but not drained. The inside was covered in moss and algae. Floating in the swamp muck were Flower of the Pond's eggs. They looked like frog eggs only with harder shells, floating on the water like scum. Inside through the filmy shell the things were looking less like worms and more like tiny versions of their mother. According to the alien she came from a swamp-like world. Seeing these it was easy enough to believe it.

Then his eyes were drawn to the softly throbbing glow of the machine. The UFO the aliens had brought in was small, barely the size of a fairground ride. Bethany and the zombies had stripped it and rebuilt it into the shield generator. It looked incredibly complicated. The alien had cursed impressively every time she found another broken piece of equipment that could not be replaced. Seeing her frustration at "this stupid barbaric planet" was almost the only good time he had since he had gotten his mind back. Bethany calmed her down by reminding her that if they succeeded, they would not need a space ship.

He twitched and looked away from the pond. The zombies were dying. Quite quickly. Their eyes could not catch whatever the women were doing to them. The others had come with guns and explosives. Slow and limited. They could kill dozens, even hundreds of zombies, but there were always more and when they ran out of ammunition…

Whatever these people were doing was different. He could almost not even sense the individual destruction of the zombies. It was happening too fast. Like watching a strobe light. Normally eventually the people he sent them after would be overwhelmed. This was more like watching mosquitoes disappear into a bug zapper.

"They are still killing the zombies," he said.

"Just keep sending them," Bethany snapped. "Tell me when they are dead."

Brock smiled like a crocodile, sending out the order. "As you wish." Sensing it as more of them were snuffed out Brock knew there was something special about this group. They were not slowing down and it was only because he had zombies everywhere that he was able to keep track of them at all. Quick steady progress, straight toward them. Part of him knew he should tell Bethany, warn her that they were coming. But she had ordered him not to, hadn't she? And Bethany's enslaved monster was nothing if not obedient to his mistress's orders.

Monster Mash

The zombies died easily at the hands of the monsters. Even Tut had shown a few good moves. Not as tough as the others she had shown a few decent moves obviously learned when she participated in midget wrestling augmented by her unnatural abilities. Sheila had been impressed to see the little woman skitter up a wall and flip backwards to land on a zombie's back, slicing out with her ceramic knife with anatomical precision to slice off its head. Sacrificing people to the gods was obviously at least as informative as a few years in med school.

Yet while they were easily dispatched, the zombies kept coming. Slowing them down each time. They traveled through the day and the rest of the night. Sometimes they stopped to loot more supplies. Food, guns, and other things. There was plenty lying around. Most of the people who would use such things were dead and the few left were in hiding, not yet desperate enough to venture too far from home for food. Not until the local groceries stores were exhausted.

Eventually as dawn came up the next day they were all mentally exhausted, if not physically. They could all conceivably go forever, but after almost forty-eight hours of running full speed from town to town and tearing through zombies, they needed a rest. Fortunately they were prepared.

They found a bowling alley, a nice solid brick building with no windows. Busting out her supplies Tut strung the doorway with red yarn and then put a line of salt across it. Either one was an effective barrier against zombies. Together when the shambling figures approached the door they stopped, reaching forward gingerly, but their hands stopped an inch from either, as if hitting a glass wall. They could hear the zombies scratching at the brick walls, but they were weak movements and none seemed to have the initiative to go search for tools.

"Same thing happens to me when I try to get into somebody's house without their permission," Queenie said, yawning. All of them could see well enough in the dark room and they had found a line of vending machines. Not everyone had to eat and they gave the bulk of it to Sheila and

Luna, but what woman could say no to chocolate? "Of course if it were me I'd have gotten some explosives or gasoline and tossed it in here."

"Don't give them ideas," Tut warned, looking nervously at the closed door.

Lying back on a bench and ignoring the smell of used bowling shoes the vampire waved it off. She wished Sheila could have curled up with her, but she barely fit herself and while she had enjoyed showing off, looking at half rotted zombie viscera had not been the most romantic way to spend the evening. She had already spent one full day on her feet and needed a bit of a break.

The others felt the same and soon they were all asleep. Not an easy task as it turned out that Luna snored quite loudly. Only she, Mary, and Sheila needed to breathe and wouldn't you know it, one out of three just had to be noisy. Yet their weariness drove them under and soon they were all out anyway.

Perhaps that noise was why it took so long for them to notice the gunfire. In fact it was only after Luna suddenly stopped snoring and sat up that the others awoke. Outside there were popping sounds that got closer and closer. Then explosions. Finally the roar of a truck. They ran to the door. The sun was still up, only a few hours having passed and Queenie flinched at the direct light, but she was too shocked to bother covering herself at the moment.

Outside were two trucks, each outfitted with a modified snowplow. In them were a bunch of men, armed to the teeth with weapons Sheila was pretty sure were illegal. When she saw what the ammunition was doing to the zombies, she was sure of it. They practically exploded even before they started tossing grenades.

"God bless America," Silk said. "You have to love people who can immediately take advantage of a lack of gun control."

Tut nodded, her delighted eyes on the men as their plows flattened zombies by twos and threes. "Think they'll let me drive one of those?"

Nobody answered and to their delight soon the whole area was cleared, one last shot ringing out as a man finished off a not quite dead enough decapitated head. They looked up at the women and began heading towards them, guns in hand. They did not quite aim at the girls as they approached. One of them, a big man with a thick beard who looked like a *Duck Dynasty* fan took the lead. "You all alive in there?"

"Close enough for horseshoes," Silk said. "Who're you guys?"

"The South Divide Militia," he said. "I'm David Phillips. Who're you?"

Sheila stepped forward, puling out her ID. "Sheila Casey, FBI."

He grinned, though it seemed a little off. "About time you government types got here. What took so long?"

"We've been here. It's just that our people keep getting eaten before they get this far."

The men shared a laugh. "Yeah, that'll happen in these parts." He looked at them, trying not to drool. "You ladies some sort of special forces?"

"Something like that. Why do you ask?"

"Because every damned zombie in town started ignoring us yesterday and heading in this direction. We followed and found a bunch of them diced up. Then we see them all trying to get in here, but they can't seem to even touch the door. And we know that never stopped them before. How'd you keep them out?"

"Magic," Tut said.

The men shifted uneasily and their hands tightened on their guns. "Magic?" David's eyes narrowed. "That mean you're responsible for all this?"

"Heck no," Queenie said. "Normal just people kept ending up zombie chow so they needed a little something extra sent in."

Mary nodded. "It's true. Someone else started this."

"Who? The government?"

"Nah, some kid goofing around with magic," Silk said. "Look it's complicated."

"How do we know you're telling the truth?" He asked.

She shrugged. "We've been killing the zombies. They're trying to kill us. Seems pretty conclusive to me."

David and the others nodded, though their eyes were locked on the girls' chests. He lowered his gun and looked at them, his eyes pleading. "Can you fix this?"

The men had looked so cool and in control before. Now… it was heartbreaking how lost they seemed. Sheila said, "We're doing our best. We have to get to the Southward Mall. You know a short cut?"

"Not just now," he said. "Sorry. The zombies blocked off most of the main roads. They aren't this smart in the movies."

"Preaching to the choir," Tut said.

"Anything we can do to help?"

Around her Sheila saw the faces of the girls light up. They began to pose provocatively and lick their lips. "Uh oh…"

Ignoring that Luna arched her back and grinned as all five men stared, a couple counting under their breath, unable to believe what they were seeing. "Actually boys, there is a little something you could help us with. You see I have this itch that needs some scratching. A hunger that needs feeding. If you know what I mean."

"Certain… needs a lady has," Queenie put in. She slapped Sheila on the ass, making her jump. "Right darlin'?"

Blowing a kiss to one of them Tut openly rubbed her small breasts and wiggled her hips. "Something you have that we could use."

To their surprise even Silk got in on it, her sunglasses focused on one at the back who looked to be maybe old enough to have graduated high school. Maybe. "Hey hot stuff, you a virgin?"

He blushed, almost but not quite stepping behind the others. The men grinned back at him. "I… I was… just… saving myself… marriage."

Silk smiled. "Well it's the end of the world and I'm pretty sure the priests and most of the other girls are dead. Why don't you come on in here and I'll show you my idea of a good time?"

"Does that leave the big guy for me?" Mary asked hopefully, bending over in the doorway to see the guy with the beard and coincidentally flashing cleavage so large and deep a man could get lost in it. He stared, gulping loudly. Then he held up his hand to show off the ring. "Sorry, I'm married." He looked at the other four. "If you boys want to help these ladies out though feel free. I'll stand guard incase any other zombies show up."

"Really Pa?" The younger once asked, his voice squeaking.

"Aw hell, it's like they said. It's doomsday. Might as well go full bore and those are some fine women. When we get back to base I'll even treat you to your first beer."

"Come on boys, we're waiting," Luna said and they backed away into the darkened bowling alley. The men were too busy stripping off their camo jackets and hurrying after them to notice the way their eyes glowed eerily in the dark.

"I don't think this is a good idea," Sheila said.

"Shut up," Luna growled. "We aren't here to rescue these people. Remember you got us into this so we could keep—!" The men arrived, spreading the red yarn and stepping over the salt line.

"Golly," the young one said. "Sure is dark in there."

"So?" Silk said, grabbing his shirt. "Come on, we'll head to the end of the lane and see if you can't get some gutter balls."

Sheila felt a wave of jealousy as Queenie grabbed the arm of a twenty-year old boy that smelled of beer and took him over to the benches. The vampire winked back at her in the dark, blowing her a kiss. Sheila looked away, blushing and indignantly grinding her teeth.

"You okay?" Mary asked.

"I'm fine."

Looking around the giant woman sighed. "Damn it, none left for me... unless someone wants to share."

Nobody looked to be volunteering. Luna grabbed a pudgy redneck whose beer belly was sticking out from under his shirt. She began fiddling with his belt. "Whoa, what's your hurry?"

She whispered in his ear. "I don't want your clothes to get stuck in my teeth."

"Well yee-haw," He said and started helping her undress him, reaching out to run his hands over her breasts. "Damn I ain't never seen anything like this even in stag films down at the lodge!"

"Oh believe me, you ain't seen nothing yet round boy." She took him behind the snack counter. "I think I found the butter from the popcorn maker..." She held a bottle in her hand that smelled of butter and oils. "I think I'll cover you in it and lick it off." He did not seem to have he words to respond.

Tut had gotten the last one, a tall guy with a lot of muscles. She smiled up at him and ran her hands as far up his stomach as he stared down at her. "You're legal, ain't ya?"

"Oh baby, I'm much older than I look, trust me on that," she slid her hands into his pants. "Let me show you how experienced I am and you see if I'm a girl or a real woman." He collapsed against the wall with a moan and she crawled onto him.

Sheila leaned against the wall by the door and stared out. Mary took the other side, watching the girls with longing. Around her the FBI agent could hear moans of pleasure, male and female. Sheila tried to ignore it as best she could. She never liked guys sexually at the best of times and had no real desire to see them get laid. She could not help but glance back at Queenie after a while though, only to see her unnaturally gray bust still beautiful body completely nude. *Maybe*, she thought, *I can join in. It's not like I have to touch the guy after all…damn she's hot!*

So Sheila was actually watching when the screaming started.

Queenie had her guy still standing, her on her knees in front of him. She had unzipped his pants and given him a hand job, getting the blood flowing until he was big and hard before taking him in her mouth. Her head had bobbed up and down for a moment until he was close to getting off, the pounding of his heart almost echoing off the walls and the blood pounding in his ears. Out of the corner of her eye she could see Sheila watching, a disgusted look on her face. Queenie could sense her thrall's jealousy and disappointment that Queenie would do something like this. She had thought the vampire loved her.

Queenie did love Sheila, but the girl barely knew her. She needed to see what she really was before committing herself. Like Sheila had said, Queenie was a bimbo. A slut. She had spent most of her life and a huge part of her afterlife fucking anonymous men for money. More than that, Queenie was a monster.

The man in her mouth was about to finish when she pushed forward, taking him deep into her throat and then he gasped, eyes crossing, as she bit down. Looking at Sheila as his jaw dropped open, in too much pain to scream, she made eye contact with the girl and held it while she dragged her head back, her razor sharp fang slicing unhindered through the meat in her mouth. She stopped at the end just long enough for Sheila's eyes to widen in shock as she saw the man's dick split open like a gutted trout. Then Queenie ducked forward again, swallowing loudly as her mouth was flooded with what she had been after all along. It flowed down her throat, leaked over her chin, and some dripped out between her lips to cross her pale breasts in thin red lines to fall from her nipples like milk.

The man started to scream out loud. In the pale light his friends briefly looked up, but all they saw was him getting a blowjob from the chubby girl.

112

Queenie had latched her clawed fingers into his ass and no matter how much he pushed and struggled he could not get her off of him. I was like beating at a statue. He could not even articulate a cry for help, just scream as unheard of pain shot through his whole body. From the way it looked to the other humans in the dark, he was having a great time.

"Oh my," Mary said, She pulled a notebook out of her coat and a pencil from her hair, taking noted. "This is fascinating…"

Suddenly there was another scream, but this was cut off quickly. They looked to where Luna had been mounting her partner, bouncing up and down in short quick hops that reminded Sheila of when her family dog used to try to hump her leg. Now she was arched back, that fat guy's hands still grabbing at her chest, his fingers digging hard into her soft skin. What had been gropes and caresses as he explored her triple sets of tits, were now white knuckled clenches that left nail marks that healed almost instantly. Luna's bottom jaw was drenched in blood. Between her teeth they saw a piece of meat briefly before she swallowed it. Below the counter and out of sight there was a pained gurgle. Smiling hugely, red animal fangs flashing, not quite fitting into her human mouth, Luna ducked down snarling hungrily.

Peeking over the counter Mary and Shelly saw her worrying the body. Her claws turning flesh and fat to red ribbons while she dug her teeth into his throat her head shaking from side to side. Her hips held him tight and to their shock his body was apparently getting in one or two last orgasms despite his current predicament. Unable to stop even as he died twitching in pain. Perhaps her claws and fangs were so sharp he could barely feel it at first. Judging by his wide eyes as the light left them faded, he could barely believe it himself. Luna meanwhile continued to hump even as the life left his body. All the while she continued to eat and shred him.

There was a whimper and they turned to see Tut, in the big guy's lap, her back to his chest. He was inside her, stretching her pussy lips open so they could see the rings piercing them and the bolt through her clit. His hands were rubbing on her tiny breasts, tugging at the rings there too. She was leaning back to kiss him hungrily as she drove herself down onto him. It seemed he did not realized what was happening to him while this was going on, too focused on the tight warm wetness that held him. In the dark he could not see the way his body was drying up wherever it touched her. His veins turning black. His skin wrinkling like old parchment and his hair turning white before falling out. Around his mouth especially as Tut was literally sucking the life from him. Riding his dick into the afterlife.

As the kiss broke she whispered, "Death is merely the beginning." He tried to speak, but his tongue was a withered black thing. Realization that something was wrong came too late and as Tut increased her tempo, bouncing faster and faster as she eagerly sucked the remains of his life force out through his balls with her vagina, he began to fall apart. His skin cracking and then his whole body disintegrating until she was sitting in a pile of dust, hands working on her own body to finish what the now very dead man could not. "Yes! Gods, I feel so alive!" Sheila remembered that he French referred to having sex as "the little death" or some such. Now she knew why.

Which left Silk, who had been taking her time slowly stripping her virgin. He had been saying things like, "Ow, watch it. You're scratching." In the dark he could not see the marks she had left. Strange symbols similar to the ones on her own skin, though not as deep.

"Don't worry, just relax and give yourself to me," Silk whispered and it almost sounded like there were other voices. Distant ones. You could almost make out the words, but not quite. He almost thought they were in his head. "What's your name?"

"J-Jimmy," he stuttered.

"You've never been with a woman Jimmy? Not ever?"

"Uh... no ma'am," he said, swallowing.

"That's good. I love virgins," she purred. She grabbed his hands, bringing them to her breasts. "Here… feel this."

Jimmy obeyed, his hands running over them and the deep cuts in her skin, tracing them at first. Then he gasped. One might have thought in pleasure, but then he tried to pull back. His hands moved just enough hat Sheila and Mary could see the small tendrils, like pure blackness, sinking into the flesh of his hands from inside the cuts. They pulled him back and she opened her mouth. He tried to struggle, but thicker tentacles shot from her mouth and to his face, sinking into the skin like worms in Earth. Jimmy tried to scream, but her sunglasses came off and his eyes locked on the vacant holes, somehow able to see them even in the pitch dark.

"My god… it's full of stars…" His jaw hung open and his eyes rolled up. Something, a light pulsing like a small star slowly came out of his mouth and into Silk's where it disappeared. Then he breathed one last time and his body exploded, spraying blood and meat everywhere.

"Amazing," Mary said, taking more notes, writing through the red spray on the paper. She looked at Queenie again. "Oh my… that certainly isn't like in the movies."

Sheila turned back to the vampire and immediately flashed back to the night they had met. When her brother had died she had seen vampires feed for real and this was just like that. As Mary said, it was nothing like the clean romantic love bites of the big screen.

Queenie's victim was on the ground either dead or unconscious from blood loss and that was a mercy. She had finished sucking his dick dry and as Sheila watched the blood that had dripped down on her seemed to ooze up her body on its own accord, as if trying to race its way into her mouth. She did not care, reaching out she grabbed his head and tore it free like plucking an apple, then she crushed it un her hands jaws open wide to catch the blood as she wrung it out. Her teeth sliced through meat, sheering off chunks into her mouth where she sucked every drop from it before she spit it out onto the floor and took another bite.

"Mmm, so good…" She moaned. Her tongue moved around her mouth in circles, licking up every red spot of blood before tearing another piece off his skull. At superhuman speeds it was soon nothing but glistening white bone before she crushed it and dove inside like it was a popcorn bucket to get the rest, spitting out chunks of brain and his eyes like watermelon seeds. Then she tossed it aside and ripped off an arm, doing the same thing as if she was juicing fruit. The bones shattered with wet popping sounds muffled by the muscles and skin. She sucked on the jagged ends, looking ridiculously like a hamster at a water bottle. She even sucked out the marrow inside, cracking the bones open to get at it. Next she did the same with the next arm, the legs, and finally she dug both hands into his chest, cracking it open like a nut and throwing the rib cage wide so she could dive face first into the cavity. Her teeth flashed and she bit into his heart and sucked it dry before going to the lungs and liver. She slurped and sucked loudly, her head bobbing like when she had been giving him his deadly blow job as she writhed in obvious enjoyment. Blood got everywhere, but all of it seemed to be alive, crawling and racing into her mouth on its own.

"This is… hideous. Horrifying. Terrible," Captain Mind Ripper said, his body shivering against Sheila's back in fear.

"The word you're looking for," Sheila told him. "Is 'monstrous'."

"Indeed," Mary said, writing it all down. "This is fascinating. She is clearly consuming more blood than she should be able to… not that humans can digest blood in the first place. Look at Luna. How much can she eat?"

Sheila looked and saw that the fat man was already stripped of meat from his bald head down to his shoulders, the werewolf woman gnawing on his skull and sucking the brain out through a rough fang-marked hole. Bits of skull crunched softly in her teeth like dry cereal as she gulped down his gray matter as if it were a gelatin mold.

Suddenly Sheila felt hands reach around her and cup her breasts. She looked around and down into Queenie's glowing eyes. Her skin was remarkably free of blood despite having been basically bathed in it moments before. Behind where she had been Sheila could see two piles, one of bloodless meaty bits and another of splintered bone shards.

"*Now* I'm horny!" Queenie said.

Sheila wanted to argue. She had seen Queenie blowing a redneck and then devouring him. Her human side was screaming for her to run. Her heart fluttered with the fear that Queenie would do the same to her. Would rip her apart like tissue and drink her dry.

Another part though, felt her connection to Queenie through whatever link they had. The vampire's normally cool hands were warm and while her heart did not beat the blood was rushing through her veins like a river, filling her with the life force it contained. Queenie truly was turned on, her body humming with the need for sex that followed the violence. More than anything else she wanted to satisfy herself with Sheila, the thing she had wanted every moment for the last decade. The same thing Sheila wanted, though she had tried hard to suppress it. Now that dam was broken.

Emotions flooding her Sheila did not need to ask what Queenie wanted. She turned around and grabbed the vampire's face, leaning down into a deep hard kiss. Queenie kissed back and they carefully slid their tongues together between her fangs, still tasting slightly of the coppery tang of blood. Queenie grabbed her zipper and pulled it down, letting her cat suit fall off while Sheila undid her bra and tossed it aside.

"I don't think you should..." Mind Ripper began.

"Shut up or I'll eat you too," Sheila said and the alien fell silent. He had seen her eat spiders before and after what he had just seen did not want to tempt her. She and Queenie fell to the ground together and began having sex. They kissed and ground together. Licked and sucked and got into a sixty-nine, looking like a yin-yang symbol. It was amazing being eaten out by a woman who did not need to breath. Queenie could suck non-stop and definitely knew how to use her tongue. Meanwhile maybe Sheila was not quite as good, but she was more experienced with women and from the happy growls Queenie gave she was doing good enough. They connected mentally and suddenly it was like a circuit of ecstasy as they felt each other's pleasure. Each orgasm shared by the other as if it was her own, doubling each time until it was all they knew.

"I've never had sex this wonderful," Queenie said in her mind. "No man ever made me feel like this."

"You should see what I can do with proper preparation," Sheila replied, suckling hungrily at her clit.

"I can't wait."

Time seemed to get away from them. Inhuman endurance and long suppressed desires kept them going until the other girls were all done with whatever clean up they needed and were watching them with interest. There was some talk of a better pool on how long it would take them to stop.

"What's that called?" Mary asked, watching unashamed as a wildlife documentary film maker.

Sheila, who was washing herself off with wet paper towels from the bathroom peered over. "From what she's doing with her tongue... I think that's called the Transylvania Twist..."

After a while the guy from outside came in. "Damn boys what's taking so long?" He stopped in the light of the doorway and looked down, his foot making sticky noises on the hard floor. He saw the blood. "What the hell?" Reaching for his belt he pulled out a small flashlight and swung it across the room. He saw the spray of blood that covered everything. He paused at the odd pile of dist, uncertain what that was. Then he saw what was left of Queenie's victim and looked like he was going to vomit. Finally his flashlight caught the women.

They were beautiful, but Luna was covered in blood. She was sitting on a bench, holding her breasts up, bending down to them beyond what a human could do even with years of yoga and licking all six of them clean and even giving her own crotch a few cleansing laps every now and again. She did not so much as glance away from the task as the light hit her. Then he caught Tut who was still brushing the dust off her naked body and Silk who had a dozen dark tentacles hanging out of her mouth, her empty eye sockets seeming to absorb the light of the flashlight. Queenie briefly looked up from Sheila's quivering loins and flashed him a smile with her white teeth that let him see her fangs shining in their full glory and dripping with her lover's essence until Sheila pulled her back down by her breasts, stretching and groping them roughly in her fever so they could continue their superhumanly energetic coupling.

"What the hell—?" He brought his shotgun up fast and fired, peppering the three not on the floor with buckshot.

Finally looking up Luna snarled with her blood stained fangs. "You son of a bitch!" The pellets fell out of the holes the had left, falling to the floor as the holes healed. Ditto for Tut and Silk. "That hurt!"

"You're monsters! You killed my boy. I'll—!"

He never got to finish as Mary grabbed him, throwing him up against the wall next to the door. "Hello big boy!" She licked her lips, standing over him and manhandling him as if he were a small child. She smiled at the other monsters. "I've got this one. I need a little lovin' myself and it's been a while since I really let myself go."

They nodded and watched like she had as she ran her hand over his still smoking gun barrel like she was jacking off a large penis. The man tried to fight free, but he could not and as she bent the barrel of the gun in her hand as if it were made of aluminum foil he froze. Looking as she stroked it with her hand and then crushed it between her fingers he let it fall from his hand and looked into her eyes to see sparks flashing behind them.

"Please… don't…"

Mary shook her head. "Sorry but Mary needs snu-snu!" She opened her lab coat and undid her pants, letting them fall to the ground. She pushed him down to the ground and reached out, snapping his belt, buttons, and zipper with one hand. "Mmm…" She straddled him, her huge body enveloping his as she settled onto him. His dick hardened in her huge soft fingers despite his terror until she moved it to her vagina, her giant clit poking him in the belly like a small penis itself. He was horrified to find that that imagery did nothing to make him less hard.

The man struggled a bit, but he was engulfed face first in Mary's enormous chest and he soon submitted, instead focusing on briefly getting his face free and gasping for much needed breath. She was beautiful and riding him like a pony and for a brief time he seemed to really be enjoying himself. She had been designed for this after all. But after a while she started getting into it and things took a turn for the worse. Mary began to moan and writhe, her legs squeezing together around him. Her hands grabbing at his body, pulling him close. His eyes widened as his mouth and nose were pressed into her deep cleavage, blocking off his breathing again. He started to black out from lack of oxygen. Which was a blessing because it also muffled his screams as Mary continued to squeeze. Things popped. Bones snapped like dried twigs.

"Harder! Harder!" She begged and rubbed on him as hard as she could, but while her flesh and spirit were willing, his were rapidly turning to pudding. It would have been kinder to lock the man alive in a working cement mixer.

He was dead long before she finished with a disappointingly small orgasm. When she finally stopped she shook her head. "I need to get back to my lab and the Sexatron-3000. Human bodies just don't have the stamina a hydraulically powered sex-toy does."

"Sounds like fun," Luna said, licking her fingers and picking a hunk of something out of her teeth with a claw. "If we make it through this, I'll give it a go. You're right, humans don't last long at all."

"Preaching to the choir sister," Tut told her, patting some dust from her thighs.

Mary went to the sink, where there was thankfully still running water. She glanced at Silk. "I thought you said you didn't do sex."

"Not as humans understand it. Gods do it in seventeen dimensions. But virgins... they're special."

"How?"

"It's all about potential," Silk said. "Human souls have all kind of power, but the unrealized potential to merge your life force for the first time with another human being in an act that not only brings you to the height of ecstasy, but can potentially create a new life... oh that sort of power is immense and almost irresistible. Properly channeled there are all sorts of things it can be used for."

"Why do you think gods and sorcerers and priests always like virgin sacrifices?" Tut asked. "It's why me breaking by vow of celibacy pissed off my gods so much."

"Unrealized potential..." Mary said thoughtfully.

Luna burped. "Come on, let's pry Sheila and Queenie apart and get going."

She stretched. "That guy was full of cholesterol and I could use the exercise

to keep him from going straight to my thighs." She looked at the remains of

the men Queenie and Mary had killed. "On the way out though, I need to

pack a doggy bag for later."

Tut smiled and jangled a couple of car keys. "I'm driving!"

Mind Ripper muttered around whatever part of Queenie Sheila was sucking

on, "You people are sick."

"We're not people," Silk reminded him snatching the keys. They

eventually got the two women apart and cleaned up, though it was not easy.

Queenie kept batting them aside and with her strength even Mary had

trouble. Potentially with their undead speed, endurance, and regeneration

Sheila and Queenie could have kept going at it forever.

Finally Luna doused them with water, making them shriek, but not stop.

"Get up or I'll get the garlic butter I found next to the popcorn maker."

Shooting her a dirty look the girls finally unhooked and got up. "Spoil

sport."

Let's Split Up Gang

The trucks had been outfitted to push the cars the zombies had put everywhere out of the way. Taking the. they plowed through the blockades. Tut laughing evilly as she pushed them aside and in some cases over the edge of bridges where one burst into a huge fireball. They made pretty good time. At least for a while. The next town over they ran into a surprising problem. After hours of slogging down the road they came to the edge of what looked like an ordinary city and to their shock, could not go any further. Silk got out and placed her hand on the invisible barrier and cursed. She pressed her whole body, squishing her boobs against it. "Lousy stinking karma!"

"What's going on?" Mary asked.

"You know those spells to stop the undead I couldn't use?" Tut asked. "Looks like someone else can."

Mary reached out and her hand passed through as if nothing was wrong. She stepped back and forth easily. Sheila did too. When the others tried that they might as well be trying to walk through a glass wall. Only they would have had more luck with actual glass.

"You're the result of twisted sciences, not unholy magic," Silk said. "Of course you're fine."

Sheila asked, "What about me?"

"You're a thrall. You're alive still and your hitchhiker isn't magic at all so no surprise there," Tut said.

Before Sheila could answer Mind Ripper spoke up. "I have some bad news."

"What is it now?"

"I smell something in the air." Sheila sniffed and she felt the alien on her back squirm around a bit, adjusting its grip. "It smells like a breeding pond. I believe the eggs are hatching."

In the mall Brock stood still by the throne while Bethany laughed hysterically. The zombies had herded most of the human captives together around the pool when Flower of the Pond had announced that the eggs were hatching. The humans had known what was coming. Bethany had told them. They had not even fought. They knew it was useless. A few had tried to kill themselves, but the zombies stopped them so they had gone along with it.

It was heart breaking to see their complete lack of hope. Of course that dead look in their eyes, barely better than a zombie, faded when the eggs hatched and the screaming began. The adult aliens apparently knew how to attach painlessly. The babies, fresh from their eggs, not so much. The eggs hatched and as they did the thing on Bethany hissed, clicked, and screeched, guiding the young as they followed their instincts, leaping onto the humans and down their backs. Their sharp little legs sinking into their skin and attaching to their spines. Then they produced webs that took control of the rest of the nervous system.

Worse was the way the screaming stopped as the little parasites took hold. The blank look on the host's face as their nervous system was co-opted. Then one by one they came forward and knelt by the throne.

"Oh this is marvelous," Bethany said. "So much better looking that my undead slaves. Mmm, there are some cuties in this group. Hey Flower, do you think I can give a couple of them a tumble? There are some tantric sex spells I've been dying to try."

"Allow them a few day's grace," Flower of the Pond warned. "We don't want to overload them right away with too many hormones before they are ready."

"Fine," Bethany said like a kid denied candy. "They will follow your orders, correct?"

"For a time. It takes time for us to develop our own personalities and I plan to teach my children the true *way* of our kind."

"Whatever," the girl said dismissively. "I just want to see if they can use any of those hardcore special ops weapons we looted from those government guys."

"I assure you, they are more than capable of that," the alien said.

Bethany clapped like an excited child. "Good! Let's get them started then!"

"So we go around?" Luna asked.

"Looks like."

"No," Mary said. "We don't."

"Why not?" Queenie asked.

"Because we're doing this stupidly. I thought so when those guys showed up to 'save' us." She looked at Sheila. "I get why you had us stick together until now. It was good for reconnaissance and we needed both my and Tut's knowledge to get up to speed on things. But we need to stop acting like humans." She looked around at all of them. "It's perfectly obvious by now that the zombies aren't a threat to any of us. They are threats to humans but who cares? Like Luna said we are not here on a rescue mission. We need to stop acting like humans and start acting like monsters. Play to our strengths. If the eggs have hatched then we're running out of time."

"What do you suggest?" Sheila asked. She did not like the idea of her hand picked team taking over, but she knew that if Mary had an idea it was probably a good one.

"We split up." She pointed at Luna and Queenie. "You two are the best suited for a quick attack. I can tell you've been holding back for the rest of us. You didn't even have to fight the zombies. You could have gotten by them easily and Queenie said she could fly if it was night." She looked at them. "You two need to leave us and see if you can kill the bitch behind this as fast as possible."

Luna shrugged. "Works for me."

"I guess. Come on Sheila, I can fly with you and…"

"No!" Mary said firmly. "We don't need you distracted. You've blown enough time on each other…"

"Hey, you did too—!" Sheila began.

"Yeah, I know," she said. "We all took some time our for R&R back there. But that was before the eggs hatched. If that was what our enemy was waiting for before they start on whatever else they have planned, I don't think we should be goofing off."

"Point," Tut said.

"Fine, so what about the rest of us?" Sheila asked.

"You and I are going straight through this town. If we can find whoever cast this spell maybe they can help us. If not, you and I are going to prepare some surprises incase Luna and Queenie fail."

"Me?" Sheila asked.

"Well technically the lump on your back," Mary said.

"Hey!" Mind Ripper snapped. "I am not a lump."

"No, you're your people's idea of an astronaut. Which means you have to have some scientific knowledge, right? Maybe not as much as your psycho engineer, but more than anyone on this planet has I'm certain. "

"Sure,' he said. "It's just… well there are rules about… you know… giving technology to… uninitiated planets…"

"Look, your people caused this and we're going to fix it," Mary snapped. "I can promise we'll do whatever it takes to make sure you don't face the blame, but now is not the time to hold back because we're uneducated barbarians. Besides, we're not human… heck technically we're all dead. So I doubt there's any rule against us getting the tech."

He nodded Sheila's head. "You're right. I'll help however I can."

"Good."

"What about us?" Silk asked.

"You two have the magical know-how, but you're our weak links. You aren't as fast as Luna and Queenie. I've seen you sprint Silk, but when you get up speed it's more like watching a puppet run and you get kind of jerky. You and Tut can't cross this city as fast as they can and you'll just slow the others down."

"So what? We get left behind?" Tut asked.

"Hey, you two both have supernatural powers," she said. "Take the trucks, get at close to the mall as you can and find a safe place and figure out something you can throw at this bitch, even if it's just a distraction. I have no idea what you are actually capable of and it's best if none of us do, because if we fail and get captured, you two are our last hope."

Silk nodded. "So you send in the power houses and see if they can kill them outright. If that fails you and the back-leech throw some high tech at them, and if you fail we're your Hail Mary."

"You got it."

"Good plan. I see they picked the good brains to slap into your skull."

Mary looked at Sheila. "Come Igor." She turned and headed towards town.

Sighing Sheila nodded. She hunched up her back, pressing Mind Ripper against her shirt like a hump. "Coming marthter!"

"Hey," Queenie shouted.

Sheila smiled. "Just kidding." She leaned down and kissed the vampire one more time. "If we pull this off you can show me who the master I'm cumming for is later."

"You know I will."

"Don't make me vomit," Luna said. "Fingers get caught in my throat on the way up."

"Prude," Queenie said.

"Dyke."

"The A-team," Tut said sarcastically as Sheila hurried after Mary.

They both turned and glared at her, but then looked up in surprise as a lone zombie came shambling onto the road from off in the bushes. They bared their claws, but Silk held up a hand. While she agreed with Mary she did not like being relegated to the backup team. She was a god for crying out loud. "You two, get going. I got this. I'm going to send our enemy a little message."

They had no idea what she meant, but the two sheathed their claws and then turned and ran, leaving them quickly behind. Tut watched them go and disappear for a moment and then leaned against the truck to watch the show. She may have had her differences with the gods, but watching them work when you were on their side was always fun and it sounded like Silk was going to do something extremely nasty. This she had to see.

The zombie, being a zombie, was not really expecting anything but if it had been having the pretty young-looking girl throw her sunglasses aside then grab it and kiss it was the last thing it expected. It tried to bite, but found its mouth full and unable to close as a river of black tentacles flowed from Silk's nose, mouth, and empty eyes into its body. It was pierced by more slithering out of the runes carved into her flesh and soon it was held in the air a few feet away as more moved into it until it was full the bursting, things moving under its skin until it looked ready to split.

Bethany Jones, evil necromancer, was still outfitting her new alien army with the best weapons the government had plus a few things her undead hordes had procured from local militia members when she felt the surge of dark power. It had found some way past her defenses. She felt her heart clench as she looked around, expecting something to burst through the skylight or even the walls. Nothing seemed to happen.

Except then Brock bent over, eyes wide. His mouth opened and black tentacles surged out. His back arched as a hideous tree-like growth surge out, each branch sprouting a hideous orange eye. They looked around in literally every direction at once, but then they came together, focusing on Bethany and merging into one huge eye. The air around her seemed to speak.

"Oroth k'u Ghuramba uroh le'ak thul-pock xenra koth!" The words vibrated the whole building... no the very air shook with each inhuman sound. The walls appeared to be melting. In fact the walls started to bleed. Some of the humans still in the closer holding cages began clawing out their eyes for a few seconds before their heads literally exploded. Brock, even though his mouth was full, laughed insanely, unable to stop even as tiny centipede-like things began to pour from around his eyeballs like tears. Behind the strange words was singing, not unlike the voices of children. Over and over she heard, "In the dark we all do play, never to see the light of day. Beyond all hope here we'll stay, along with little Bethany."

On her back Flower of the Pond began the shake, gibbering incoherently. The only thing protecting her was the aura of dark magic Bethany had and

136

that was a thin protection at best. Nearby two of her children and their hosts fell apart, each piece of their body crawling away at it morphed into unidentified slithering *things*. Bethany could feel the thing before her trying to get inside her mind and soul. Not just her head, but her soul. Tainting her with a presence not meant for human understanding. That was never supposed to exist in this universe.

Yet she stood, fighting back. She had gone deep, deep into the darkest pits of evil magic. This thing was powerful and wrong, but it was beyond concepts of good and evil. Blessings and damnation. Things she had reveled in. Like so many other things these were foreign concepts and in some ways worse even than this creature, with its infinite capacities, could contemplate. At once too great and too small and focused for a creature that swam in the depths of infinity. Its presence was corrupting the entire world at the moment. So it could do nothing as she staggered forward, placing her hands on Brock.

"Be gone! You are unwelcome here!" She snarled, forcing her own dark energies back along the line, severing the thing's connection to the servant she had created. "This one is mine!"

The tentacle was severed. Cut off from the source it fell from Brock, melting and rotting before it even hit the ground. The eye popped into viscous fluid that began to eat through the floor. The black flesh made of pure darkness and corruption melted away showing surprisingly white bones underneath before they collapsed into dust. Soon aside form the hole in the floor, the thin rivulets of blood coagulating by the walls and the dead bodies of a few of her captives, there was no proof it had ever been.

Brock was still laughing, but Bethany was pissed now. She forced him back to sanity, looking through his mind. Her consciousness crawled around inside him making him scream and soon he settled down, breathing heavily. In her mind she saw the things he had not told her. Saw her mistake in his orders that let him hide her enemies.

"You fool. You still defy me."

"However I can," he rasped.

"Never again. So ordered."

"Yes... mistress." He said falling back to the ground.

From her back she felt spasmodic twitches. Flower asked, "What... what was that?"

"That was an annoyance which I will have to deal with," she snapped. She went over Brock's mental images. So a vampire, a werewolf, some kind of very powerful demon, and a handful of other things she could not identify had come to her island. It was almost like a bad joke. Her eyes were drawn to the far end of the mall, where the special cages were, each one containing a different individual kept separate from the others for special uses. Between her and them was a complicated symbol that her minions had carved into the ground. Deep enough to catch the blood that would fill it.

"What are you going to do?"

"Various things. First of all, summon your children. I'll need them to gather supplies from the jewelry stores, the cooking stores, and the furniture store. Now! Then I'll need someone to bring me one of the special prisoners." She hated to do this. A virgin was a terrible thing to waste. But that had been a serious slap across her bows. "Brock!"

"Yes," he hissed from where he lay.

"Pull your zombies back from the little one and the one with the symbols carved into her skin," she said. "At least until I can deal with them. Surround that protected city and make sure those other two cannot leave. I don't know what they are doing in there and I don't like surprises I'm not behind."

She barked out more specific orders. The zombies and aliens moved to obey. Soon one of the cages was empty and a pretty young girl was dragged towards her. She struggled, but the alien-hosts holding her did not care. Following Bethany's orders they stretched her out on the floor in front of the throne. She squirmed in their grip, but to no avail as Bethany approached her.

"Sorry to use you like this," she said. The girl screamed as Bethany held up a long curved knife. "But someone is messing with my plans and I need a little help if I'm going to stop them."

"Please, don't... aaaaiiieeee!" The girl screamed as Bethany made the first cut.

She ignored this and the screams that followed. She carved symbol after symbol into the girl's skin, cutting through her clothes and exposing her nude body. Blood flowed freely, forming a pool around her. Brock watched from where he was, leaning up to see. With her other hand Bethany drew symbols in the blood which seemed to writhe and glow. She circled the girl whose attempts to escape slowed as she bled out.

When it was done and the light began to leave her eyes Bethany plunged the blade into the girl's heart and suddenly she changed.. Her skin stretched and her body grew. The bones under shifted and her face changed. She was still physically the same girl Bethany had been torturing, but you would not know it to look at her. Her breasts and genitals swelled grotesquely, the hilt of the dagger still sticking out above her left nipple more like a stud now than a deadly weapon. Her foot turned to cloven hooves and her skin went blood red. Horns burst from her skull and a barbed tail sprang from beneath her body like a snake.

The demon's eyes snapped open, blood red with cat-like black slits that seemed to draw you in like you were falling into an endless pit. She spread her claws, which shot off sparks as they scratched the ground. She rose to her feet, the ground cracking under them. Then along her skin the symbols of binding Bethany had drawn in the girl's blood appeared, glowing like fire. The demon snarled with a mouth full of shark-like teeth, but slowly knelt to one knee before the necromancer.

"What do you wish of me, mistress? For the price of your victim's soul you can order me to do one act before I return to the Pit."

"I have enemies on this land," she said. "They have summoned something from the outer realms. Find it and bind it so that it may not do me harm. Destroy any who stand in your way." She pointed. "Go. It was last at the edge of a city protected by magic not far from here."

The demon nodded its head, large horns and breasts bobbing in unison. "It shall be done." Then it vanished in a puff of red smoke.

Staggering to his feet Brock stared at the spot the demon had been in abject horror. It's hoof prints still glowed on the marble floor. "Bethany... what have you done?"

"What I had to do," she said. "Nothing can stop me from achieving my goal. Not even creatures from Hell itself."

Silk and Tut raced across the ground as fast as their stolen trucks would go. They had to catch up with the others if they could. After Silk had done whatever she had to the zombie, she had dropped it and Tut watched it decompose before their eyes. Silk had not been interested. Instead she had sprouted a thousand more eyes and began looking in every direction, muttering under her breath. The sun had set and the stars were coming out. She was watching them intently.

"If the Dog Star is there and Mars is there with its moons rising then..." She counted on her fingers and then sprouted several hundred more tentacles to count on. "Counting the position of the comets and the asteroids against the black hole in that galaxy... shit!"

"What?" Tut asked. "What is it?"

"I know what the necromancer is really planning. The zombies and the aliens... Mary was right, it's a distraction. Even getting off the planet... if that was ever her goal then it's fallen to the side. I know what she's going to do and it's the worst thing possible."

"What is it?"

"Carved into the floor behind her… I saw a symbol and in the distance she had cages full of virgins. A few dozen at least and more than she'd need, though I doubt she'll spare any for this." She retracted her tendrils and met Tut's eyes with her empty sockets. "She's performing an ascension ritual!"

The mummy's jaw dropped. "Impossible…"

"No. On the night of the full moon in three days at midnight, she'll complete the spell."

"But an ascension ritual… it would take more time than a human would live just to do the calculations to be sure when the stars are aligning. It takes cults centuries just to try and only a handful have succeeded in human history. It's hard enough figuring out a time to summon something from Outside, let alone create it. I doubt even with today's technology they could do it in less than fifty years just to contacts a god or demon willing to tell them how to do it… provided thy had nothing better to do when the hole was opened. You know most of your lot have lives of their own to lead."

"How about with the technology of an advanced alien space ship combined with some occult knowledge?" Tut felt the bottom drop out of her stomach. Finding the right cosmic moment and preparing were the hard parts. "Trust me, if she's the least bit competent it'll work at the time she's figured out and since she just exorcised me from her wight, I'd give that a pretty good shot."

Tut cursed under her breath. In ancient Egyptian. Several nearby plants burst into flames and the ground was tainted for the next thousand years. The alien invasion was bad, but that was something they could fight. They were still trapped on the island for the moment. An ascension ritual… if completely correctly… would make their enemy unstoppable.

Since the aliens had hatched there had been no time limit so who knew what the others would do on their way to their goal? Maybe they would get in and out, but there was a chance they might get distracted. "We can't reach Mary and Sheila now."

"Point, so we try like hell to catch up with the others and make sure they don't screw this up."

Which was why they were now driving like hell around the city as they tried to catch up to either the werewolf or the vampire. Unlikely, especially if Queenie was indeed flying, but it was their only hope.

It was too bad they would never make it. Because as they rounded a turn there was a flash of red smoke and a twenty-foot tall demon stood in front of them. The trucks hit her legs and the front folded in like paper cups. Both the elder god and the mummy hit their heads on the steering wheels, bending them beyond use and then the demon reached down and tore the tops off the cars.

"Damn it," Silk muttered. "I've seen enough movie to know that cars are no damned good in a horror movie." She looked up at the towering demon that was smirking down at her, crushing the metal cab roofs in her clawed hands. "I can see your who-ha!"

"My master bids your capture, unclean thing," she said.

"I'm unclean? You're from the fucking Pit! You roll around in the shit of fallen angels and the damned then eat the things that crawl within it for fun!"

"A girl needs a hobby," the succubus said. Tut began shouting a banishing spell, but half way through a huge red hoof crashed down on her, silencing her. "Quiet! We're talking."

"You're going to pay for that," Silk said. "My kind never forget a sleight and when I eventually get my tentacles on you, which I will, I will do things that will make your lords in Hell scream in their sleep for eternity just to contemplate."

The demon blanched. "I only obey orders old one. Once a soldier always a soldier. Besides, surely by now you understand her plans. It's better I think to stay on her side should she succeed, for in the eternity it takes you to find a way to bring your full form into this universe, she could be a much more imminent threat than you." The demon bared its claws. "Shall we battle now?"

Silk ran a tendril over her lips. There was a chance she could defeat the demon, but she doubted it. She could see the spells that allowed the creature to inhabit its form and was admittedly impressed. She was firmly bound to Earth and that body she was in. Not like the flimsy spells that were Silk's own tenuous hold on this universe. Even this creature of the Pit was more at home in a mere four or five dimensions than she was. Any powers she summoned to destroy its form and send it home would destroy her body as surely as if she sat there and let the demon crush it. Either way she would be banished back to the void, possibly never having a way back.

"Not just now," she said to the succubus. "There's no Jell-o wrestling pit. No paying audience. So why fight?" She spread her arms and lowered her head. One thing an eternity in the formless void beyond time and space teaches you, is patience. "I surrender."

The demon laughed and scooped her up, its hand wrapping around her and lifting her into the sky as if she were a doll. She turned and vanished into a puff of smoke.

In the crater left by the demon's foot Tut's smoking body was knitting itself back together. She stiffly crawled out of the hole, muttering under her breath. "Stupid damned demon! Unfair! Damned necromancer! Crush me under her foot will she?" She sat up, broken bones rattling like rice in a bag. Her eyes blazed with unholy anger. "Didn't even bother to take me, huh? I'm the weak one? Not a threat? I'll show you! I'll show you all!"

The curses of the ancient Egyptians were known to be pretty powerful and long lasting. They also say that Hell has no fury like a woman scorned and that a person with nothing to lose was capable of terrible things. Combining them all into one small form, Nafertut intended to prove all three. Just as soon as she could feel her legs again.

The Best Laid Plans

They say that any plans you make in war never survive the first engagement. This is especially true when your enemies know all your weaknesses and that you are coming. There was, after all, a reason that vampires and werewolves did not rule the planet. After a brief break along the way Queenie and Luna split up as they approached their destinations, street signs easily leading them to the Southward Mall.

Queenie arrived first because as soon as the sunset she was able to levitate and fly there. She wished she could have done it with Sheila in a Superman/Peter Pan kind of romantic way, but Mary had been right about keeping them apart. Too bad.

She landed on the skylight above, peering down inside. The power was still off but aside from her ability to see in the dark the walls were lined with generators and lights from some of the stores. There was a gold throne and behind that a large ornate bed that had probably been dragged out of another part of the mall. A teenage girl was lying on it playing video games on a laptop. Around her were maybe a dozen zombies and even more shirtless humans, gray spiders about a quarter of the size of Mind Ripper attached to their backs lugging huge weapons around with them. Off to the side a hideous creature, pale as death with blank white eyed, stood against the wall looking bored.

The edges of her fingernails glittering like razorblades she reached down and used them to cut a small circle in the glass, easily catching it as it fell out and set it aside. Closing her eyes she let her body dissolve into mist and began to seep into the building. She had been momentarily worried about getting in. The mall was public property, but they had been living there a while. She had feared she would have to go to the front and talk her way in.

As she worked her way down from the ceiling Queenie tried to decide who to attack first. The wight controlled the zombies. On the other hand the girl controlled the wight and the alien on her back controlled the other aliens. Besides the girl smelled delicious while the wight was as unappetizing as the zombies. So she drifted towards the bed, hovering above it until she was ready to—

"Now!" The girl snapped, rolling away just as Queenie materialized and slashed down. She barely missed, her hands sending up a puff of feathers from the mattress instead of blood. She snarled and tried to follow, but it was too late. Three of the alien hosts whipped around and leveled their guns at her. Queenie stiffened, expecting to be hit with bullets. Instead she barely had time to realize that they were squirt guns before she was hit with pure garlic juice.

"Gah! You bitch!" She stumbled back, preparing to try shredding anyone in her way, but then she saw that those surrounding her were covered in yellow powder. More garlic. Her senses were going haywire, her eyes watering until she was blinded. She turned back into mist and tried escaping upwards, back the way she had come. But They were ready for her and they herded her until she found herself floating into a bottle. Before she could back out they plugged it with a cork.

Queenie's senses were not much in mist form, but she felt the bottle move and heard the girl's voice say, "Sorry about this, but I can't let you and your friends interfere with my plans. Just a couple of days and—"

Brock cleared his throat, interrupting Bethany's rant. "Sorry mistress, but the other one is coming. She's tearing through my zombies like they are nothing."

Guns turned towards where he pointed and they all looked just in time to see Luna burst through the front doors in her partially transformed state. She was naked and looked like an escapee from furry convention. Bethany and Brock froze, unable to keep from taking a moment to stare at her triple breasts. Not something you saw every day.

Fortunately for them, neither the zombies nor the aliens cared much about human anatomy and she barely killed six before the rest started blasting away with everything they had. Luna was strong, but even she buckled under the assault of dozens of guns all aimed at her and firing continuously. She fell back, one arm blown off, a leg barely held on, and her whole body riddled with more holes than a termite mound.

She looked dead for sure, but even as Bethany took a step forward to see if she was finished, the bullet wounds started to fade, spitting the slugs that had not passed through back out onto the hard floor. Her leg reattached and her arm literally slid across the floor as if magnetically attracted and came together with the rest of her at the stump.

Whole again Luna sat up and glared at them, her eyes glowing an evil yellow and her lips pulled back over wolf-like teeth.

"Second wave, fire!" Bethany ordered.

Some of the alien hosts stepped up, leveling shotguns. Luna sneered at first. If solid bullets had not done anything what made her think pellets would do better? But then they started shooting and she barely had time to see the shiny glitter in the air before her body erupted in literal fire. Bethany had loaded the shells with silver from the jewelry store. There had been bullet making equipment in one store and loading in tiny chain links and more had been easy.

Wherever they touched the werewolf her skin burst into flames. White like lightning, as if from firework sparklers. Luna screamed in an all too human voice, falling down and writhing on the ground. The world was nothing but pain. Then Brock the wight came over, a large meat cleaver in his hand. "I'm really sorry about this." He raised it and brought it down, slicing off her head. "Well that's... holy hell!" Luna's body continued to move, clawing at the ground under her. The heat from the fire was melting the silver, which was dripping out of her banking the fires. And while her head stayed separate, her neck was throbbing and it looked almost like... "Her head is growing back!"

"Shit," Bethany said. "Okay, shoot her again and then we need to get her locked up."

"You awake yet?"

When Luna came to, her whole body smelling of burnt animal hair and cooked meat, she was lying in a small cage. Having wasted one virgin to get the demon to trap Silk, who was ten feet away and sitting in a large circle that glowed on the floor, they had a spare. Absently the elder god stuck out a finger to the edge of the circle, but stopped when red sparks flew out of her finger. Luna growled and sat up, looking at her surroundings. She could have torn the cage apart, except they had super glued silver jewelry all along the bars and top of the cage. The sun was shining through the skylight above and reflected off the metal into her eyes.

"Ouch," Luna said, covering her eyes. "Damn... I hate when they cut off my head. The new eyes always take a while to get used to bright light." Her nose and ears were both overloaded too.

Silk pointed to her empty sockets. "I know what you mean." Then she nodded to a large green bottle on the floor not too far away. Inside something moved around like fog, swirling angrily. "Right now Queenie isn't really in a position to compare."

"So much for our great 'kill her while she isn't expecting us' plan."

"Yeah, I think that fell apart because she was totally expecting us."

The werewolf peeked through her lids. "What are you doing here?"

"Got kidnapped by a demon," she said. "Who then brought me here and held me in place while little Miss Sunshine over there built a containment circle."

"I thought you were a god," Luna said. "Couldn't you do anything?"

"Sure, but it would have turned this planet into the solar system's new asteroid field and would have destroyed my body, banishing me back to the outer void. I'm saving that for a last resort."

"Ah." Luna looked around. "Where's the shrimp?"

"Last time I saw Tut, she was being ground into the pavement like a cigarette under the demon's hoof," Silk said. "After that I lost track of her as I was carried off."

"Great. I hope the others are doing better than we are."

"I doubt it matters." Silk said, poking at her prison. "When I was caught I was trying to warn you. I found out what they're working on."

"What is it?"

"An ascension ritual." The werewolf stared at her blankly. "Look gods like me just come into existence. Some gods are born. Other gods create some. A

154

few are mortals who reincarnate after really proving themselves and are born to gods as children. On the other hand some of you cheat by using an ascension ritual to force yourself into that position on this level of existence and when it does… well continents sink, holes are torn in the nature of reality, and worlds tend to get devoured in the process."

Luna glared. "You seem awfully calm about that."

"Hey, I'm eternal. I'm trying to stop it, but if it happens I'm sitting back and watching the show." She looked at Luna. "You seem to be pretty hard to kill too."

"Yeah, I'm sure I'll do fine when the Earth is destroyed. You know, floating in space up until I get sucked into the sun."

"Nah, you'll be burned up before you get there. People seriously underestimate the point of an O-zone layer. Hey I wonder if you'll regenerate if your chest does that exploding thing," Silk said. "That'd be so cool to watch in zero gravity."

"So glad you'll be amused as you float around like a space baby in the debris of my home planet," Luna snarled. Her stomach growled. She yelled out to the zombies and aliens across the mall. "Hey, when do we eat?"

"You don't," Bethany said, smiling nastily. "I'm keeping the food and extras for the humans I'm using as sacrifices. You three are useless. I'm also not cleaning out your cage, so you'd better learn to hold it or you'll go the same way as my hamsters and my brother's gold fish." She snickered. "And my brother come to think of it."

Luna sneered at her. "When I get out of this I'm going to eat you like a chocolate bunny so you can feel every bit of it as I work my way into the middle."

"Yeah, good luck with that," she said. "Two more days from now and you won't even be a threat." She turned away, ignoring them.

"So..." Silk said. "Twenty questions?"

Luna groaned and slapped a hand over her eyes. "Can't the world just end now?"

The B Team

The protected town where Mary, Sheila, and Mind Ripper found themselves was actually pretty nice. There were a lot of people around and they eyed the odd strangers as they walked around, but so far nobody had attacked them. Mary led the way to the nearby University and they paused as they saw down to the football field. There was a large symbol painted there, guarded by a lot of large men with big guns.

"Like it?" A voice said and they turned to see a thin black girl watching them, smiling brightly. She had her face painted up like a skull, a top hat and a back coat on her back. In her hand she held a black walking stick. Under it she was wearing a bikini.

"What is it?" Mary asked.

"The symbol for protection against zombies," she said. "My grandmother taught me how to do things like that. She used to live in Haiti and knows all about the weird stuff that has been going down." She looked them up and down. "I'm Janna, who are you two?"

"I'm Sheila Casey, FBI. This is my consultant Mary." She flashed her badge.

"FBI? Really?"

"Doing what we can," she said.

Mary nodded. "I see you lot have things mostly handled around here. Any chance you can show us to the school's research lab?"

Janna nodded. "No problem. Especially if you're here to fix things."

"We'll do our best," Sheila said.

As she turned and led the way Mary asked, "Did your grandma teach you any spells to protect you from… oh let's say fire?"

"No… why?" Janna said.

"Just curious," Mary said and shared a look with Sheila, both of them thinking of the missiles that were still prepped to be fired on the island should the shield come down. "So this lab, is there a generator?"

"Yes, but we don't use it much except when we're cooking lunch for the guards. Got to conserve after all."

"Well tell whoever is in charge that conserving is over. If we fail, you're all dead anyway."

"Why? We've been safe so far."

"That was before the aliens hatched," Sheila said. "Unless you have a spell for them, trust us they'll be able to walk right through."

"Aliens?" Janna turned and stared at them. "What are you all into? First zombies, then you weirdoes, and now aliens?"

"I won't put up with you calling her a weirdo," Mary said with a straight face. Both of the other women stared up at her for a moment. "Look, unless you can stop every zombie on this island right now, we need to get to the lab so we can work on it and don't have time to clue you in." They looked hopefully at the girl.

She sighed. "Wish I could. I had to offer up some promises to the Baron just to get this place protected from the walking dead."

"Yeah, we know a god too," Mary said. "They can be really skimpy with the whole 'protecting mortals' thing." They walked to a building near the edge of campus and Janna stepped away to talk to some people.

When she came back she said, "We'll have the generators over here and running in half an hour. We've got a few solar ones we've been saving and enough gas to last maybe a couple of days." She smirked. "Not like anyone's driving any more."

"Excellent," Mary said. "Any researchers around who could assist?"

Janna shrugged. "Sorry, it took everyone a few days to realize the zombie thing was serious. Only a small part of the town is still alive plus people who came here and found shelter. A lot of the students and teachers died early on when the authorities asked them to investigate what was going on."

"Okay then, just make sure we have some privacy then," Mary said. "I'm going to be pushing the bounds of science and I'd hate for anyone to get hurt. It limits the available test subjects when I've finished." With that she and Sheila hurried inside the empty building, their feet echoing around the dark hallway as they made their way in.

Eventually they found a decent lab and the power was up. Mary scanned the computers and Sheila found herself sent to fetch chemicals, lab equipment, and other things from storage. Soon the lab looked like something out of a science fiction movie as Mary brought out vials and things hidden about her person. No machinery. What little she had brought from her own lab had been abandoned when they came to the island.

Not that it mattered because she began assembling more with impressive speed. Mind Ripper used Sheila to relay information and answer Mary's questions, but it was not easy. As advanced as she was Earth was a long way behind the Mind Lord and other species. She could probably reverse engineer most of their tech if given a year or two to work with, but as it was most of it even an on power sources that were beyond them. She understood most of what the alien explained, but it was like knowing how to build a television when you only had rocks and sticks to work with.

In between she borrowed some medical equipment and began scanning Sheila and Mind Ripper's biology, their connection to each other, and what she could do about it. The alien told her, "I'm not sure how I feel helping you develop weapons against my people."

She raised an eyebrow. "Then you should have stayed off our freaking planet. Look, it's not like we're going to wage war on your people. We're stuck here, right?" He had no response to that.

Sheila in the mean time assembled weapons she could from other chemicals. The locals were not giving up their stockpiled weapons. They had been through a lot and most were unsure how well or long Janna's spell was going to last. She had no idea what Mary was actually doing so she could be no help there, so instead she worked on bombs and other explosives. There was plenty to work with and her training at the FBI had taught her about such things. Not exactly bomb squad material she still knew the basics.

The next night though, Sheila suddenly stood up, eyes wide. "Queenie is in trouble."

Mary looked at her. "What?"

"I can't explain it, but I feel like she's in terrible danger. Our connection... I don't know why but it seems foggy somehow. Like trying to connect to mist... but I know she's in trouble."

"What could they possibly have done to her?" Mary asked. "I mean we sent them on ahead because they were unstoppable. If anything happened to them it should have killed her, not just put her in danger. What could they do to a vampire? Unless they have crosses, garlic, running water, rose thorns, fire, wooden stakes..." She paused. "You know it occurs to me that vampires have a lot of weaknesses and pretty much everyone knows what they are."

"Shit." Sheila grabbed a backpack she had found in the schools lost and found and began loading it up with bombs. "We got so used to fighting zombies we forgot that anyone with a brain knows how to deal with vampires."

"And werewolves," Mary said. "Oops."

"Are you done here?" Sheila asked.

Mary shook her head. "I'm doing the bare minimum. I have some ideas on how to override the alien control and maybe even take over the zombie's bodies, but that would take weeks. As it is, it'll take me time to finish anything even at my level in time to do any good. You should probably wait."

"I can't do that," she said.

"No, I suppose not. I understand the imperative to obey your master. Do what you need to." She paused. "Hey Mind Ripper, we can probably snag you another host from the people around here."

"I can't just force someone…"

"Bah, I'm sure we could find a volunteer."

The alien paused. "No, I'll go with Sheila. I'm not sure how much help I've been to you, but I think we've hit a wall. Maybe… there's some way I can defuse this situation. Flower of the Pond is one of my people and maybe I can reason with her."

"Good luck with that," Mary said. "In my experience genocidal zealots aren't usually easy to talk out of things. But maybe that's just humans. I'm sure that an advanced alien culture like yours is completely different."

Sheila spared Mind Ripper having to answer by lifting the pack and heading for the door. "Do whatever you need to do to take care of this mess Mary, even if it means nuking this island with us on it." She looked over her shoulder. "Like Luna said this isn't a rescue mission. Our goal is to kill off the aliens, the zombies, and whoever is behind them. If we fail the whole world dies. Remember that."

"And you should remember… don't jiggle that bag too much or it could blow you straight to Hell."

Wincing and then gingerly scooting out of the door so she did not hit anything Sheila nodded. "Yeah, I'll be careful."

The mall was close and with her able to cut through the town Sheila should have been able to get there easily, but not far from the edge of the town she came across a patrol. Large men in a Mustang pulled up to her and piled out. It occurred to her that a lot of them men she had seen among the survivors were the burly macho type, but then she realized that only made sense. While geeks might know more about zombies, being able to run and fight were skills you would need to survive in this sort of situation.

"Hey girl, where are you going?" One of them men asked. "You're getting close to the edge of town."

"The zombies are even worse in that direction," another said.

"I know," she said. "I'm on a mission to help some people."

The leader shook his head. "Lady, if they're out there they are probably dead."

Sheila debated telling him that Queenie had been dead before, but saw no point. "Not my problem. I have to go help." She started forward and they all moved to block her. Four of them all armed to the teeth.

"Sorry to tell you this, but you can't leave."

Sheila frowned at them. "Why not? It's my life."

"Because we need you here," he said. "This little community… may be all that's left after all this craziness. There's no way to tell if or when the zombies will get off the island and if that happens… well we all know how that works. We can't afford to let a pretty girl like you just walk off and get killed."

Sheila pulled out her badge. "You have no choice. I'm an FBI agent and I have authority here."

They peered at the badge and then their boss snatched it away and tossed it over his shoulder. "Fuck that shit. Like the government has any power here. If they did they'd be in here with tanks and guns and we wouldn't be forced to be hiding out in this little burg under that crazy voodoo girl. So just turn your ass back around and head back into town."

Sheila sneered. "Or what?"

The man smiled. "Well, seems to me you need both feet to walk out of here but not to have kids." He cocked his gun.

"Fuck you," Sheila said calmly.

He grinned. "Hell, why not fuck all of us?" The guys behind him laughed and they started forward. Sheila lashed out, sending him flying back into the car. "What the hell."

"Don't make me hurt you," she said.

"Get that bitch," he ordered the others.

As they advanced Sheila considered her options. She could fight them. More than one very well trained law enforcement official had sparred with her and regretted it. She was a great fighter and with Queenie's supernatural gifts she had a definite edge. Then she remembered the weight of the bombs on her back. Having and edge or not, she could not afford to risk bumping them too much.

"I'm warning you to back off," she said. They ignored her, sure that they could easily take the apparently unarmed blond who looked lime an immature teenager fresh out of high school.

"Should I handle this?" Mind Ripper asked.

"No, I got it," she said.

"Playing crazy isn't going to help—!" The leader said, getting back to his feet.

Sheila nodded. "I know." She had been hoping to get through this without getting blood on her hands. She had joined the FBI to help people. And considering that only a few thousand out of the seven million people on Long Island were alive and it had been weeks since this disaster had started, she had seriously not expected to have to deal with any deranged humans.

It was not that she had gone her whole life without seeing anyone die before or on this trip. She had once shot someone when she was part of a raid on a den of drug dealers. Plus she had sat by and watched as the team she had hand picked had devoured half a dozen men who had come to their rescue. Hell she had given orders to Mary to destroy the island and everything on it if that was what was needed.

Yet here she was pussy footing around these bastards who were standing between her and Queenie— uh, saving the world! "Screw it!" She stepped forward between them, startling the men and making their leader back into the car again. She grabbed his gun and unceremoniously tore it from his hands. While they looked she swung it around, pressing it to the leader's head, and pulled the trigger. She did not even flinch as his head exploded, splattering her face and clothes with blood and brain goo.

"What the hell! You just…" The second man did not even finish as she swung the gun around and blew his chest apart. The third was bringing his weapon up when she did the same to him and the fourth was still staring in shock as she crushed his face with the butt of the gun.

Gathering up their weapons and securing ammo from inside the car she walked off, bits of them still dripping off her as she walked. "Sorry boys, but I cut you all the slack I could. I don't have time to deal with you dumbasses."

As she headed out of town Sheila thought about what she had done. It was one thing for monsters to kill humans. They were supposed to and needed to eat them. Or at least had lived so long that they probably had a split with humanity, seeing them as short lived and unimportant. Sheila on the other hand was still young and had no desire to eat humans. Though the way she felt about rats and insects was probably similar.

She was immortal too, the blood slave of a vampire. Was it any better just sitting back and watching Queenie squeeze out men like oranges in a juicer? Was it really bad killing them when she was trying to save the world? Her superiors were prepped to turn everyone here to ash the second they had the chance. It was also only a matter of time before that town ran out of supplies too and those guys probably would have been the first to be sent out to look for more in the zombie infested towns around them where they would inevitably die. What did it matter if she shot them first? Should she feel bad for even being the type of person who would ask that question?

"Are you okay?"

"I'm just remembering something the shrink they sent me to when I shot a drug dealer a while back. I realize now why after a few decades killing humans seems so unimportant to the others. Thinking too much about something you have to do, even if it hurts someone, is just torturing myself for something I can't control. I came here to save the world. If those punks had to die it was a small price to pay."

"What about the others? When this is over will you kill them? They're a threat to humanity too aren't they?"

She should, she knew. Those monsters were worse than any serial killer and had higher body counts. Maybe the zombie queen and her aliens had somehow caught Queenie and presumably Luna too, but regular cops who were not expecting them would never be able to stop them. If they even believed they existed and considering how long they had been working undetected by most law enforcement that seemed unlikely. Did she have the right to allow that to continue just because she was in love with Queenie?

"I suppose I can justify letting them live unmolested two ways. One is that they would probably just slaughter whoever came after them," Sheila said.

"And if they were found out it would cause a panic. There's a reason we're keeping the zombies under wraps. How would your people react to this situation?"

"I have no idea. I suppose it depends. If Flower's people were handed control of it they would be ecstatic. Mine too I suppose. But to have it suddenly dropped on us with no understanding of what it was or where it came from. We'd be terrified beyond reason. I… to tell the truth I can barely comprehend it. It's like when I tried explaining my technology to your friend."

"My friend." The sex obsessed cyborg killing machine designed by a mad scientist working for the government.

"You said there were two reasons not to turn them in."

"Well if this goes off right, they'll have all helped save the world. There isn't really a prescribed reward for that, but I did get them into this on the promise that they could keep eating people. Comparing maybe a few people a year against the seven billion they are saving… well you can't measure one life against another, but a few lives against all of them seems fair." She shrugged. "Of course if we fail it becomes moot."

"True. So do you have a plan? Apparently killing zombies and heading straight in the slaughter everyone was a bust."

"Then we'll have to do what humans do best." She smiled, drying blood spots flaking off her face. "We're going to be sneaky."

In her head she came to a realization. This was not the kind of horror story where the plucky humans fought the monster and won. This was the one where two monsters faced off and the humans were caught in the crossfire. One monster and maybe a few humans would live. The rest died.

As she thought of how she felt making love to Queenie and imagining an eternity of the same, Sheila decided she was okay with that. Her FBI shrink would be so disappointed with her.

So it was another day before she could make her move. She made her way to the mall and spent hours until dawn watching the "people" around it. She had looted some binoculars. The mall did not have many windows. They were designed that way just like casinos and stadiums. Even the skylight was tinted. It kept the light from interfering with any shows they were putting on and people from telling how long they had spent inside blowing their money. Unfortunately in this case it turned the mall into a nearly impenetrable fortress and the zombies guarding it along with some healthier shirtless people with large spiders on their back, were a daunting sight to say the least.

She caught glimpses inside two ways. One, by positioning herself so she could see through the doors. Not a great view, but they opened frequently to let patrols in and out and she caught glimpses of a blue haired girl on some kind of golden seat and cages behind her at the far end. There were people in them and she thought she recognized Luna. Everything else was out of her line of sight.

The other glimpses she got were from Queenie. This close their connection was stronger and she could feel the vampire's distress as if it were her own. The images she got were foggy, as if she needed glasses, and seemed tinged green. Whatever the reason she could sort of make out Luna behind bars strung with cheap jewelry and to her surprise what looked like Silk sitting near by looking bored. Had she betrayed them? Sheila also got a look at the blue haired Japanese girl and the freaky man-thing with her that was probably the wight.

She considered trying to take a pot shot through the doors, but gave it up. The guns she had were not sniper rifles and this close to the horde a miss would only let them know where she was. Absently she moved her shoulders, letting the weight of the bag she carried settle down on her. She slipped it off and looked inside, taking a mental inventory. Three time

172

bombs. The rest were radio detonators, all rigged to one control with a red button that just begged to be used.

"Do you have a plan?"

"I have a plan and a backup plan," she said. "But first it requires us getting one of your kids over here with us. You ever heard of the story of the Trojan horse?"

"No."

"Then do you know anything about subterfuge?"

"I am from a species bred for subterfuge."

"Good, then this should be easy."

Brock had held out small hope for the monster women stopping Bethany, but now the toughest were captured and the others had been no where to be seen for a while now. With Bethany's new and more specific orders he could not have kept them secret from her any more anyway and she would just send the zombies straight to them. The little one had been crushed anyway and the other two were either still in the protected city (most likely) or stupidly sneaking around somewhere off the beaten path. Mostly he just saw zombies, the occasional squirrel and every now and then some poor doomed schmuck out scrounging for food that the zombies would shortly take down.

So he was surprised when just off the edge of the mall parking lot out in the bushes that led to the nearby park, something exploded. He immediately turned and reported what the zombies were seeing to Bethany.

"Shit, more? Is it their friends?"

"No idea," Brock said. "For all I know there are a dozen more teams and the one we know about was just the big distraction or something. What should I so?"

"Send some zombies out and…" She pointed to one of the alien hosts. A bald middle-aged man with a beer gut hanging over his belt. "You go too. I want someone with a functioning brain to head out there. Besides I'm sick of looking at your fat ass." He went without comment, not having understood her, only Flower's orders.

"If you feel that this host is unappealing you can use one of the others. Some of the ones in the separate cages… I still do not understand the need for them in all of this. What possible difference does it make if they have produced young or not?"

"I've explained this. Virgins, especially females, who are capable of giving life but who have not yet done so represent… potential. And if I… we are to become gods, we need as many of them for the spell as we can get."

174

"I am not sure how I feel about that part of your plan. I came here to serve my people's god. The force of the universe that allowed us to escape and overtake our creators and which will one day allow us to control the universe in an unstoppable wave of peace that will end all war as we assume our rightful…"

"Yeah-yeah, enough with the rhetoric." Bethany said and pointedly ignored the sarcastic snort that came from Brock's direction. "Look, you can either serve your people's faceless, unknowable god who may or may not exist… or you can be their god. Be the immortal all-powerful being who leads them in universal domination. People won't need to be conquered. When they see you, they will bow down and declare you their rightful lord and master."

The alien shifted on her back. "I am still uncertain if I believe you capable of such a thing should I go along with it."

"You didn't believe I could raise the dead either. But you saw that. Then you saw me summon that demon and capture those monsters. You should show a little faith."

"Uh mistress, the zombies I sent to check out the fire are being shot," Brock said. "I can't tell from where but the others are hearing the bang just as someone's head explodes."

"Flower, what about your child?"

"I'm not telepathic," the alien said. She moved Bethany's eyes to Brock's. "What can you see?"

"Well he's still alive and… damn, there goes the last one I had over there."

"Send more," Bethany snapped. "We're two days from the new Christmas and I'm not letting anything get in the way. Build a wall if you have to but figure out what's going on!"

Zombies had begun to converge on the spot when suddenly the side and back walls of the mall exploded. Bethany screamed and ducked down, displaying that despite everything she was still a teenage girl. Brock would have liked to let her die in a hail of shrapnel and fire, but that was not an option and he found himself throwing his body over her protectively. The zombies left the fire outside and came to the mall, which now had gaping holes in two walls.

"What is going on?"

"I don't know," Brock snarled.

"My children are crying out. Their hosts have been shot. There's an intruder near the virgins."

"Shit…" She looked up at Brock's blank eyes. "Anyone over there?"

"Only a couple and none too close. They were coming to protect you."

At the other end of the mall Sheila snuck through the large hole she had made. She had used one time bomb for the distraction outside and had plans for the second. The last was in her hands as she snuck in; the radio controlled ones having been used to blast her way inside. She made her way in quickly ignoring the two dead boys in the cages closest to the hole and the others who were begging her to save them. Instead she made a straight shot to where she could see Luna and Silk.

"Are you two okay? Where's Queenie?"

Luna shook her head. "Aside from trapping us here there's not much that bitch can do." She nodded to the bottle on the floor nearby. "Queenie is in there."

Sheila blinked, visions of Barbara Eden dancing in her head. Then she shrugged and pulled out a revolver, took careful aim, and shot the bottle. Mist poured out, solidifying in the air.

"Free at last!" Queenie said, stretching. "Thanks babe."

"My pleasure," Sheila said, lustfully eyeing her body.

Silk snapped her fingers. "Hey necrophiliac, stop staring at her tits and get us out of here."

Sheila looked at the other two. "What do I do?" She tapped the circle on the floor with a foot.

"Break the circle and I'm free," Silk said. "Get an ax or something."

"That'll work for me too," Luna said. "Unless one of you can pick a lock." She pointed to the silver draped padlock on her cage.

Before she could respond Queenie screaming loudly interrupted Sheila. She turned just in time to see what was approaching her. There were two of them. Huge, pale gray, and completely inhuman with ten limbs thick like an alligator's. They looked like a cross between scorpions and rhinoceroses. The mouths were round sucker-like things with needle-like teeth and the eyes were blank white orbs. Only they had twin spikes on their long smooth tails, not stingers and while they had pincher-like claws from their backs were two tentacle-like appendages that moved with precision. Bethany was riding the second one, whose tail swung around and slammed into Sheila's chest, impaling her.

"No!" Queenie screamed. Her face morphed, mouth stretching and teeth changing into rows of sharp fangs, her eyes glowing like the fires of Hell itself. She looked like the vampires from the original *Fright Night*. A twisted inhuman thing that made even the demon Bethany had summoned up seem cuddly in comparison. "Not her!"

In answer one of the monsters slammed a wooden stake made from a broken chair leg into her chest with a tentacle. Queenie froze for a moment with her hideous jaws open in horror. In her mind Sheila heard her indignation as she saw the *Ikea* sticker attached to the side.

"Sorry, did I forget to introduce you to my friends here? They came in on a crashed spaceship and were pretty messed up so I made them wights." She patted the back of the one she was riding on. "They're very loyal and used to being bossed around. They make much better slaves than Brock. Too bad they aren't human and can't make zombies from them yet, but once the rest of the aliens get here they'll be quite useful. In the meantime they make good muscle."

Spitting up blood Sheila felt her legs collapse under her. Behind her Queenie hit the ground with a thud. Looking at the aliens she could see how Mind Ripper would have fit on them almost invisibly. It made the alien body snatcher's looks make more sense. If they were a few shades darker, he would have been practically invisible.

She looked over her shoulder, hanging from the spike in her chest. *Sorry Queenie*, she thought. *I couldn't save you.* In her heart that was what she really wanted. She could admit that now. From the start it was all about her, though she had been reluctant to admit it even to herself. From the moment she had realized the seriousness of the problem she had known that she could finally return to the place her brother had died and face... face...

179

"Damn it," Luna said as they watched the tail flick aside, sending Sheila flying into the still in tact wall where she splattered against it an slowly slid down in a river of blood. "I was just starting to like her too."

"Plus she was about to save us," Silk pointed out as Bethany and her two alien slaves stomped off.

"Let's hope Mary has something better planned."

Looking at the unmoving vampire lying on the ground in front of them Luna said, "That or she left us here to die."

Old Monsters Never Die

Things were looking pretty grim in Mudville to say the least, even from Silk's perspective. True when the world ended she would merely take the small portion of her being back from the host into her own dimension. But being in this dimension had been fun and an escape from the eternal void she was used to. Oh and her friends were likely to spend their own eternal lives as either Bethany's slaves or as a test to see if her new godlike powers could in fact kill them.

Sheila's body was left against the wall where it had fallen, battered and broken. Queenie still existed inside her staked body, but she was too far away for Luna or any of the caged virgins to reach and the zombies were watching so it was pointless to even try. Plus the alien wights were stalking the mall on patrol incase they needed backup.

Luna had gotten fed at last after spending almost ten hours shouting "I'm hungry! Hungry! Hungry!" until Bethany finally gave in. The wights, all three of them, would every now and then pick a victim from the cages to suck their life force dry. The bodies were left pale, with gray lips, twisted expressions and their eyes rolled back into their heads. Usually those were turned into zombies, but Bethany had Brock dismember one and toss it into the cage with her.

"Tastes like jerky," Luna said around a mouth full. Bethany watched with interest as she devoured the dried out meat and began gnawing the bones like a dog.

"I don't suppose you lot can have sex in this situation?" Silk asked the people in the other cages. "It'd really help if you were not virgins."

"We've tried while she was sleeping," one girl said. "She's been telling us all about her plans so we thought it worth a try to foil her. It didn't work, even though most of us are teenagers and can still get excited in this situation. We're too far away from each other to even give a hand job let alone anything really intimate." She jerked a thumb at the boy in the next cage. "I almost reached the tip of Danny's dick once, he's pretty well hung, but he came up short and when we masturbate it doesn't seem to bother the bitch."

"No, it wouldn't," Silk said. "I'd help you if I could but..." She reached out with a tentacle, but it flared into ashes at the edge of the circle.

"Thanks," the girl said, trying to hold down her look of fear and disgust. "I'm not really into living through one of those Japanese horror cartoons."

As the days passed and turned into hours before the spell could be performed, hope sake even more. Would they ever be saved? Or would Silk spend the last of her time in the mortal world watching zombies shamble around?

Bethany had called in the entire horde. From what she said there was a sea of zombies stretched out around the mall. Several million of them, forming a wall that would not allow anything through. The alien hosts had been split into two groups. Two hundred of them armed and backing up the zombies. Another two dozen were dressed in robes and taught a chant that Bethany had them repeating non-stop from dawn on.

"Damn that's getting annoying," Luna growled.

Silk shrugged. "The chanting is important. It creates a vibration in space that allows for..." She paused, looking at the bored werewolf who was probably thinking about food again. "It makes it easier for the spell to work."

"Would killing them interrupt it?"

"No."

"Shame." Suddenly her hands flicked out and six knives she had managed to carve with her teeth out of the body of the mans he had been fed flew, out. Two aimed directly for Bethany's throne. It may have been painted gold, but there was a chance that with enough superhuman strength behind it the knives could penetrate the same way a piece of straw could pierce metal in a tornado.

Sadly Brock's arm lashed out, taking the hit for his mistress. The knives stuck in him and he winced. Apparently wights could still feel pain. The other four hit some of the cloaked figures. Two in the back, right where the parasites were. The other two in the front, killing the hosts and making the spider-creatures jump off even before they hit the ground.

Bethany peered over the seat to look and frowned. "Now you're just being petty." She nodded to her guards and they retrieved two more humans, who screamed in terror until the aliens had taken them. They then put on the dead men's' robes and took their place as if nothing had happened. "Just for that, I'm not feeding you any more."

Luna did not reply. Brock managed to get the knives out and again time passed. The sun set and soon it was dark. Around her Silk could feel the supernatural forces of the human universe focusing, being aimed by the symbols and channeled by Bethany's spells and the chanting of the aliens. The walls of the world were thinning. Had she been free she could have stolen that power, but the necromancer knew her stuff. Whatever spirits had taught her had been good and most likely banished by the girl when she was done with them. She was way too immature to be possessed by some centuries old spirit— but then again look at the girls Silk was hanging out with? Honestly if Bethany had not been completely set on this apocalypse thing they might have all hung out together. Then again Silk preferred having incompetents in her cult who were not capable of sending her back to the void.

It was almost ten when in the distance they heard explosions and Brock looked up. "Beth, we're under attack again! It's the big one! And damn is she making mince meat of the zombies."

"Let me see," she snapped. Reaching out she touched his bald head and he grimaced as she used him to watch the fight. "What is she riding on?"

"No idea," Brock aid. "But I want one."

"Shit! She's coming right for us. Flower, have your kids on the roof shoot her down." There were flashes and bangs from the sky light as the hosts up there began firing rocket launchers and then guns. More explosions sounded, closer than before.

"She's using our technology," Flower said with Bethany's lips. There was a brighter flash. The sky light cracked as a body fell through, landing with a thud at the foot of Bethany's throne. It was half burned away, the wounds cauterized as if by fire.

"Well what have we got?" Bethany snapped. "Fire!" More flashes. Closer explosions.

"She's got a shield..." Flower sounded speculative. "Wait, this may be good."

"What? Why?"

"There's no way that in a few days anyone on this world can replicate our power sources. If we keep hammering at her she'll run out of power quick."

"Then keep firing," Bethany said. They did. Alien lasers flared in the night. Zombies and human hosts and even a few alien spiders died.

"That did it," the alien roared triumphantly. "The shield is down!"

"She isn't slowing... duck!" Bethany dove behind her throne and Brock hit the ground.

A wall exploded and in rode Mary, bits of masonry falling over her as she entered the mall. She was riding a motorcycle, but it had been severely modified. There were blades alone the edge dripping with gore from a lot of zombies. Weapons stuck out all over it. Oh, and it was also flying. Two glowing discs could be seen under it, apparently allowing it to hover in the air.

"Sorry I'm late," Mary said, smiling. "All the cool corpses were gathering here and I just had to see what was going on."

"It's a dead man's party," Bethany said, standing up. She snapped her fingers. "Leave your body and soul at the door."

The two wights came running along the walkway of the second floor, screeching like banshees. Mary raised a gun and fired, but the blast of light just knocked a hole in one, not even slowing it down. She jumped aside, abandoning the bike as the creatures leapt. They hovered for a moment, but their combined weight dragged it to the ground. Meanwhile Mary landed, her feet cracking the floor as she did and took aim.

Brock stepped up. "Sorry, but I literally can't let you hurt her."

"Too bad." Mary fired. Bethany had already moved, so she was not there when the last shot of Mary's alien-designed laser punched through his chest and the throne. In fact it made it all the way through the far wall and into the distance. The gun had several lights on it, all of which stopped glowing.

Brock looked down at the hole and then up at her shaking his head. "Lady, don't you know guns almost never work against the head monsters?" The hole was already closing in his chest.

Mary shrugged. "Worth a shot." She flipped the gun around and swung it like a bat, smashing it into the side of his head. His jaw was dislocated and teeth flew. She did not wait around to see, turning and running back to the cages where Luna and the others were. A good thing too because the guards were suddenly pouring ammo into he spot where she had been moments before. Fortunately zombies were pretty slow on the reflexes and the aliens hosts were only human.

Looking back over her shoulders Mary saw a new problem. The two huge monsters that had extradited themselves from the remains of her motorcycle were quite fast and catching up, running through the barrage of bullets like it was a rain storm. "Crap!" She turned back and smiled at Silk and Luna. "I saw all the zombies coming here and decided to make my move."

"Mary, get me out of here and I'll handle the two big ones," Luna said as she approached.

"You sure?" she asked, even as she ripped the door off of Luna's cage, the silver on the bars meaning nothing to her.

Eyeing the two monsters she licked her lips and nodded. "Oh, I'm sure…" Her words trailed off into an inhuman growl. Luna had been right earlier when she said that nobody could mistake the half-human form she turned into with her true transformation. Mary and even the zombies and aliens had to stop and stare as Luna took on her true monster form. The undisputed queen of the werewolves. The victim of dozens of curses all gathered in one individual.

Luna's human body fell back, her front splitting open as two huge hairy arms rammed their way out of her stomach. She split open as the thing inside her began to crawl free. It was enormous. Far too big to fit inside Luna, yet there it was. Shredding her body as the lupine head followed the arms, teeth the size of human fingers gleaming in its snout. It rose up, until it towered four feet above even Mary's impressive height. The humans in the cages behind her and even Bethany all had a simultaneous bowel movement as the animal part of them let them know they were in the presence of one of mankind's few remaining predators. Even the other monsters in the room, save Silk, felt a brief flare of all too human fear.

"No wonder she eats so much," Mary said, eyes wide.

Luna was enormous, her clawed paw-like feet still sitting in the tattered remains of her human corpse. Eyes like soup bowls glowed yellow under a heavy brow. Her body was covered in glistening gold fur. Her shovel-sized hands were tipped with knife-like talons. A fluffy tail stuck out behind her, wagging eagerly. Her black and wet canine nose twitched. Luna's six breasts seemed smaller on her new frame, though her nipples stuck out and even the smallest set was now bigger than Mary's. Her genitals, clearly visible, were almost an afterthought, for what creature would dare get close enough for them to matter? She snarled, the sound echoing off the walls like thunder.

Bethany managed to choke out a command. "Kill it!" The guns fired and the wights ran forward.

Luna ignored the bullets, even the few remaining silver ones as they flared in her skin and then melted free as she burned. She had eyes only for the two approaching undead aliens. The three of them came together in a meaty thump and began clawing and biting at one another. Normally the huge werewolf would have shredded any adversary, but the unnatural creatures were nearly as strong and the two together were stronger.

After a moment it became clear that they were at a standstill. They were tearing each other apart, but at the same time they healed so fast that by the time they got past one another's defenses the damage they had inflicted

190

healed. Blood and flesh flew, but in what looked to be a pointless struggle of titans. Three immortals doomed forever to battle eternally.

"Hey, stop watching the show and get me out of here!" Silk snapped. She had seen eternals battle for… well… eternity. Compared to some of the god wars she had seen this was hardly a distraction.

Mary turned to her while their enemies tried to figure out how to get past the dueling giants. "How?"

"Break the circle," Silk snapped.

Mary shrugged and slammed her fist down, shattering the floor and the circle drawn in it. Silk laughed and stepped out while the room shook. "Yes!"

"No!" Bethany said, the sound of the cracking building catching her attention. She reached under the throne's remains and handed Brock something she had made earlier, a special branding iron. She had been unwilling to use it before because it would have meant entering the circle with Silk, a suicide mission at best. Now that she was free… no reason for pussyfooting. "Use this on her. Or she'll probably possess you again. Oh and have all the zombies attack them."

"All of them?"

"All of them."

Brock licked his lips. Silk was bent over Queenie, tugging on the stake in her chest. It came out with a wet sucking sound and her eyes snapped open. He had seen what these things could do and out of all of them, even worse than what Bethany had done to him, he did not want Silk's otherworldly tendrils inside him again. Defiling not just his body, but his soul too. Hell itself was preferable to what that thing could do to him.

Using his own supernatural talents he ran forward, straight through the battling trio of monsters. He dove between their feet, sliding across the slick floor and then rose up, less than ten feet from the others. As they helped the vampire to her feet they were distracted by the wave of zombies fighting their way through the doors and the holes in the wall left by both Mary and Sheila's entrances. So he had time to rise silently behind them and plunge the branding iron down. As it approached Silk even though it had never been heated it flared red, flames flickering over the metal.

Silk barely had time to turn as the hit iron contacted her left breast, sizzling on her skin. She made a sound that set the walls to bleeding again and then backhanded the wight, sending Brock flying across the room and into Luna's destroyed cage. "You son of a bitch!"

"What did he do?" Mary asked, glancing from the approaching zombies to the mark smoking on Silk's chest.

"It's a binding brand." She winced. "It's holding my power inside my body."

"Can't you get it off?" Queenie asked. "I'll rip off your tit…"

"No! With this thing on, if my body is damaged too much I can't fix it," she said. "And it's magic so even cutting it up wouldn't work any more than ripping out your fangs would make you human." Tentacles sprouted from the cuts on her body and she turned to look at Brock with her empty sockets. "I'll swallow your soul and spend eternity digesting it!"

Brock tossed aside the brand, which was already melting under its own white heat. He stepped forward out of the glittering cage, extending his claws. "Bring it!" He hissed like a radiator. Behind Silk the zombies had arrived and Mary and Queenie had to leave her.

The angry god started forward, but then stopped and shrugged. "Screw it. You kill him."

Brock blinked. Despite having no eyes he had the feeling that she was looking behind him. He was pretty sure if he was watching he could dodge her whip-like attacks from those black tendrils. If she was bluffing he would be looking away. No, she had to be faking it, there was nobody left to fight. "I'm not falling for—!"

Suddenly his chest exploded, white claws on the tips of bloody fingers having punched through his rib cage. Pinned on an impossibly strong arm he looked over his shoulder. "You... you're dead!"

Sheila smiled, revealing interlocking rows of almost human teeth, each now sharply pointed. She ran her tongue over them and said, "You know, I believe I am. Lot of that going on around here."

Queenie turned, eyes wide. "Sheila?"

"Hey babe," she said. "Miss me?" She wiggled her fingers in Brock's chest in a girlish wave. "Uh... what m I exactly?"

"A ghoul I think," Mary said. "I did some research on the trip down here. It's sort of like a thrall... actually I think vampires kill their thralls to make them into ghouls. Pretty much the same only more... undead than alive. They feed on bugs and rodents like a thrall, but also dead animal and human corpses. The more rotten the better. I guess to clean up after their vampire masters. They feel no pain, heal from anything but complete decapitation and having their body burned to ashes. They're supposed to have fangs and claws that can cut through stone, the better to get at bodies inside tombs and can open their mouths large enough to swallow a human head."

"Let's see," Sheila said. As Brock tried to jerk free, feeling somewhat like a cross between a pinned butterfly and a ventriloquist dummy, she brought

194

her other hand around and pressed it to his neck. Smiling inhumanly her mouth stretched wider than was possible and she opened her jaws wide, like a bear trap.

As he felt her claws severing the tendons in his neck and saw the world go black Brock closed his eyes and smiled. "Thank you!" Then his head was severed from his neck and Sheila began to chew.

Stepping back she let his body fall to the ground, bits of bone and brain turning to chum in her mouth, she swallowed and stepped over the destroyed wight. Undead had risen from tombs, graves, and coffins. Very few had ever risen from the stomach. She swallowed and burped loudly.

Queenie did not care for this lack of decorum, running forward and throwing her arms around Sheila. "I thought you were gone!" They kissed deeply, tongues intertwined. Sheila liked to think it was mostly just for the kiss and not because her lady love was licking the remains of the wights blood from between her teeth. Their fangs clicked together, sending up sparks.

"Actually I woke up the day after they killed me," Sheila said, holding Queenie tight. "But you were down and I didn't hurt… so I thought I would bide my time and see what happened."

"Good call," Mary said. A zombie came up behind her. Without looking she backhanded it, sending its head flying.

"Congratulations, you're a walking corpse," Silk said. "Welcome to the club. We meet on Tuesdays at the YMCA. Of course that requires that there be any more Tuesdays so if someone wants to help with this shambling horde of zombies…" Around her the walking corpses were falling to pieces, still obeying Brock's final order from his mistress to kill them. Or maybe they were just the closest victims and they would turn on Bethany later. Looking embarrassed Queenie and Sheila abandoned their attempt to tattoo each other to one another's skin and stepped up to claw their way through the shambling dead.

"I thought the necromancer was the threat," Mary said.

Sheila looked up at the ceiling. "Not until midnight and that's not for another two hours."

"So we win?" Sheila said. She slashed her new claws at a zombie, sending up a splash of rotting blood and flesh. Without thinking she brought her hand to her lips and licked some off. "Yum!"

"Provided we can get to her before she can sacrifice the virgins and complete the spell, yes," Silk said.

"Those virgins?" Queenie asked, pointing to the cages sticking up in the sea of zombies in front of them. "The ones she can't reach?"

Silk grinned, more zombie practically exploding into confetti around her. Looking back she saw the aliens with the weapons still held back by the fighting monsters. Some zombies were coming through, though a great many were being stepped on. They were blocking any possibility of getting close. "Yes!"

"So do we save them?" Sheila asked.

"Too impractical," Mary said. "If we fail she'll just recapture them and this hardly seems the time for them to uh… disqualify themselves. Zombies are not much of a turn on. We should kill them now."

"Easier said than done," Queenie said. "There are too many zombies and they keep popping in more as soon as we slaughter them. At this rate we'll still be trying to get close when she has a couple of zombies in the back start killing them at midnight." She sliced another zombie in half. "Hell even if we killed them all we'll have to dig through the piles of zombie bodies just to get at them."

"I have something that can help with that," Mary said. "I used up all of my explosives getting to the mall, but I brought a couple things from home that can stem the tide a little, at least from behind us."

"Do anything at this point," Sheila said. "I have an idea myself." She disappeared as more zombies cut her off from the others.

"Sheila?" Queenie called.

"I'm—!"

"She's fine," Silk said. "They're just zombies." They could see Mary pushing her way through the crowd, but then she was too far away for even her head and they were distracted. The zombies were biting and clawing at them, but Sheila could not feel it and was healing almost as fast as they could mark her. The others were barely being touched, but as they said the army kept coming and the bodies were piling up. There was some trouble keeping their footing in the chunks of pus dripping meat under their feet.

Mary ran over the zombies like an NFL football player going up against children. She stuck near the wall and barely managed to get by Luna and her opponents. A tail spine clipped her shoulder, revealing machinery under her skin, but the wound quickly sealed itself as she ran on. Bethany started to run, but Mary ignored her, instead turning around and heading up a nearby escalator. Half way up she turned and looked down at Bethany, smiling prettily and blew her a kiss.

"Hey girly, lets see how magic holds up against science." She opened her stained lab coat and reached inside pulling out a test tube. Inside were six seeds. She poured three out into her hand and returned the tube to its pocket.

"Shoot her," Bethany ordered the aliens. They raised their weapons. About six of them fired. Not one of them managed to hit Mary. The air filled with clicks.

"They used up their ammunition," Flower said. "Nothing was supposed to live long enough to get this far."

"Pity," Mary said and threw the seeds. They flew through the air and landed in the fountain with tiny plops. "Five… four… three… two… feed me Seymour!"

"Run!" Bethany said, pointing to another escalator closer to the front door. "Upstairs!" The aliens followed her lead.

They just made it as the green tendrils burst from the fountain, flowing over the floor of the mall like water. They were followed by what looked like pods or flowers, each lined with thorny fangs. They vines swelled quickly, each as thick as a man's leg and with saw-like rows of spines over them. The pods hissed, growing until they resembled the head of a tyrannosaurus.

The zombies did not get the retreat order and they fell into the plant's clutches as they mindlessly tried to get to the battling monsters. The vines whipped around like Silk's tentacles, slicing most to bits as the pods, drawn by movement, bent down to bite the few that still staggered on. They attacked anything that so much as twitched and Mary knew the more the plant moved the more it would need to eat until nothing around it moved. It was far enough away from Luna and there were enough zombies that it would be busy for a while, but it had effectively put a cork in one side of the attack.

Racing up before the aliens could reach the top floor Mary went to the cages and pulled out two other vials. The humans inside stared out at her, unsure what to think. "Okay, here's the deal. You're all going to die… but if you drink what's in these vials, then six of you will get the chance to take a few of them with you." She held them out to the bars. "Take it or leave it."

To their credit hands reached out and snatched the vials instantly. Two women took sips and then passed it to some of the burlier men. One of them, wiping a bit of whatever it was from her lips, asked, "What did I just drink?"

"Ever heard of a guy named Hyde?"

She turned and ran as the army of aliens approached her, brandishing swords and knives purloined from the mall. Mary might have been able to take them all easily, but it would take time and there were hundreds of them. Bethany told them, "Don't everyone go after her, it could be a trap."

By the time she said "trap" the door of the cage with the people Mary had given the vials to burst open and half a dozen shaped stepped out, shoving dozens of the aliens and their hosts overt the railing. The ones that has passed by looked back in horror. The figures were barely recognizable as humans. Not as bad as Luna, but they were each about eight feet tall with ape-like builds. Their clothes had ripped off and the others in the cage with them had been crushed by their bulk on their way out. Their eyes glimmered with rage and blood lust and they laughed, a combination of something animal and the mad giggles one would imagine from Sweeny Todd as he slit his next throat.

Mary called to Bethany, "I love the classics. I also have a potion that brings out the best in people, but that seemed a little useless here." She disappeared up to the third floor as the six monsters began wading into the army.

These new monsters were not as resilient as the undead and while the beasts fought with all the frenzy of their caveman ancestors, they were still sadly mortal and after only killing a dozen of the enemy or so, they were quickly skewered. Bethany smirked as their bodies fell. "A shame we can't use them for your children. They would make excellent hosts."

"Indeed," her alien passenger said. "Can you use them?"

Extended her hand Bethany sent her senses out. Then lowered it, disappointed. "No. Whatever she did to them changed them from human too much. I'd have to make a wight first and we don't have time for that."

"We should run," Flower said. "Take those we have and flee."

"No," she snapped. "No, we'll get our virgins back and complete the ritual."

"Can't we do it later?"

"Not unless you want to wait another thirteen centuries," she snapped. "Planetary alignments don't just happen."

"So we'll find another planet," Flower said. Bethany chewed that over. True, if they could get in touch with her people and go with Flower's original plan, they might have another chance any day on another world. "Come on. My children can breed and we'll have a better army next time. If we can just survive a month we'll be unstoppable, even by these freaks."

"I suppose... what are they doing?"

Down below Sheila and the others had gotten a bit of a break as the zombies bottlenecked themselves in the hole. They had been stripped of their clothes in the fights and their nude bodies glistened with body fluids of all kinds from head to toe. Now that the plant monster was taking care of the ones from the front of the mall they had fewer enemies and were wiping them out. Still it was a long way to the cages with the humans huddled inside.

"I have an idea," she called out over the crowd. "Queenie, can you clear a path around here. I need to find something on the floor and then get it to the cages."

"For you, anything," Queenie said. She rose out of the zombies, flying above them. Silk was in a circle of zombie parts as she continued to cut them up. Sheila was surrounded, but it was like an adult in a pile of children. Annoying, but not much of a threat. Below her feet the zombies tried to reach up to grab the vampire, but they could not fly.

"Get them," Bethany yelled at her followers. "Use the garlic." Most of the aliens had garlic powder on them, but they were too far away to stop what happened next.

Vampires were well known for their shape shifting powers. Wolves, bats, owls, and cats just to name a few. If you believed all the stories and movies there was nothing they could not become. Not just one animal either, like a werewolf, but dozens of them. Queenie had spent most of the last century in America, from back when it was still mostly prairie. So her choice of forms reflected that as her body broke apart into ten dog-sized ferrets. They stayed in roughly a human form for a moment, but then she broke apart and they began going after the zombies with all their unnatural speed and strength.

Too low to the ground for the gathering aliens to aim, all they could see was as the zombies began to disappear from the crowd, dragged down like they were being attacked by sharks in a pool. A circle without any moving zombies began to open up and Sheila scanned the floor, digging through twitching body parts.

The aliens took a few shots at her, throwing knives until they bristled in her back like some kind of metal porcupine, but Sheila did not seem to notice and kept digging. Finally she found what she was looking for, still on the floor close to where her body had fallen a couple days earlier. The last time bomb she had brought with her. "Found it!" She set the timer for thirty seconds and then threw it overhand, into the middle of the cages. "Silk! Queenie! Out of the pool!" Around her the other two saw the device and heard the ticking.

"No!" Bethany shouted as the elder god and the wave of undead ferrets turned and ran from the horde, no longer intent on fighting their way to Bethany's intended victims. The zombies, being brainless slaves, did not even register what was happening and simply followed. Up above Bethany reached out, trying to gain control of one to find the bomb, but it had sunk in among all the others. So she turned to her remaining wights. "Forget the werewolf! Save the virgins!"

Disengaging from the fight they tried, but Luna was not having it. As they tried to scuttle past her she grabbed their tails and held on, looking like a water skier as she was dragged over the piles of entrails soaking the floor. She let out a sound that could have been a laugh and then dug her toes in, pulling harder and dragging them away.

The bomb went off, blasting a hole in the zombies and sending more flying. It turned the ages into shrapnel and one of the bars from Luna's hit her in the arm, making her bust into flame with a pained animal sound. The alien wights were blown aside and she staggered back, clawing at the bar until she could yank it free and toss it across the building. From up above Bethany could see that the blast had been more than enough to kill her sacrifices.

"Damn it all!" She screamed, sending a blast of black fire down. It was a close up spell and meant to sap the life force from its victim, so it washed over the undead girls as if it were nothing, leaving them smelling of barbequed zombie flesh.

"What now?"

"Now we get the hell out of here," Bethany said. "We'll head up to the roof and use the fire escapes to get down into the crowd. Let's leave them to fight the zombies and my other pets. We'll make a run for it and start over somewhere else with your children."

"Finally," Flower said.

"Keep an eye out," Bethany warned. "The big one is still around."

"You mean me?" A voice said and Mary stepped out of a nearby shop. In her hands were two buckets that smelled heavily of chemicals. "You can try attacking me, but it won't do any good."

Descending and Ascending

"What are you doing?" Bethany asked, eyeing the buckets nervously.

"A little chemistry. See, it occurred to me that while your aliens might or might not be affected the same way as us in certain ways with those nanites in their systems, they're still riding humans and as far as I'm aware you are one too. You're the only one here who needs them alive. We don't. So here's a quick quiz: what do you get when you mix bleach and ammonia!"

High school chemistry finally had real life applications. "Chlorine," Bethany hissed. She turned. "Run!" Flower of the Pond sent out a signal and her babies grabbed Bethany, moving her like a stage diver at a concert as behind them Mary poured the two buckets together.

The aliens left behind dropped like flies. As Mary guessed the actual spiders were unharmed by the gas, but their hosts were choking and dying as the chlorine gas ate through their lungs. Without a dispersal device though, despite her bravado, Mary knew it would only affect those that got close and Bethany, along with far too many others, was disappearing, followed by the spiders. Mary stepped on as many as she could, but with the dead and dying bodies in her way there was only so much she could do.

"Get back here you little cow!" Mary yelled. Bethany flipped her off without looking back and they continued their egress. Looking down at the others Mary cried out. "Little help!"

"We're kind of busy!" Sheila called back. She was trying to bit the tail off one wight while the ferrets had latched onto its legs. Free at last from two opponents Luna was taking care of the other. Silk tried to help by grabbing it with her tendrils, but when she latched on she found herself flung into the zombies again like a human wrecking ball. So she let go and went back to killing them.

The white she and Queenie were attacking finally fell an Sheila jumped on it, digging her claws in. She tore chunk after chunk out of them, tossing it aside until she was literally inside its body, ripping her way through it. She had bitten the tail off and Queenie was chewing its legs off, so it could not fight back. In desperation it rolled over, trying to crush them, but it was useless. A moment later Sheila burst head first out of its belly.

Looking around she said, "Well this is ironic." Then she severed the rest of its body in half. As its insides spilled out she saw something sort of familiar, though she would have expected it closer to the head. "Hey, I think I found the brain!" She grabbed the thing, stuffed it in her mouth, and bit down. She had spent decades feasting on vermin and had even been taste testing zombies, so this was not even the grossest thing she had done in the last few minutes, let alone her life.

Like with Brock it seemed to do the trick and the alien suddenly stopped moving. Queenie's ferrets chewed a little longer, just in case, but when they got no reaction they let go and moved together, melting into one giant ferret and then morphing back into her human form. "Yuck! It's going to take a while to get that taste out of my mouth."

"Luna, smash its brain! It's in the middle!"

Whether she heard or not the huge werewolf was pounding her claws into the weaker monster, as if she were crushing the world's biggest cockroach. Its skin and bones were holding out for a moment, but without the second wight the alien undead was no match for her. Luna's claws cut through its tough hide and her strength slammed it down, breaking bones and crushing it into the floor.

Seeing no way to catch up with Bethany at his rate Mary climbed up onto the railing. In her head her brain did the calculations in seconds. "Luna, heads up!" The werewolf looked and then backed up as Mary jumped, diving feet first. The monster looked, if you could tell, surprised as its enemy backed away. It never even saw Mary coming as her heavy body hit it like a guided missile, punching through its back and smashing its brain out its belly into the floor where it became a blob of goo. Around her the alien dropped to the ground, no longer moving.

"Great," Queenie said, decapitating another dozen zombies, "Four hundred down. Six million left to go."

Pulling herself out of the corpse Mary grumbled. "Bitch and moan. Bitch and moan. Can't you contribute something positive to this situation?"

"Sure, now that the main threats are out of the way. You, Silk, and Sheila hold the zombies back. Luna!" The other three did not even question it, forming a circle of death around the two of them. The werewolf turned. "Time for plan B!"

"I love plan B! What's plan B?" Sheila asked.

"Call in the cavalry!" Queenie said and closed her eyes. Sheila felt it as she sent out a call. Meanwhile the giant werewolf raised her head and opened her mouth, letting out a howl that shook the building to its foundation and made the zombies stumble in their approach. Then they turned and started fighting along with their friends. Under them the floor was about two feet higher and made out of still moving body parts. Several minutes passed as the only sound was that of tearing limbs and groans.

"What the fuck was that supposed to—?" Silk began.

Up above they suddenly heard tapping on the roof, as if Santa and his reindeer had landed. From outside the hole they heard howls, answering Luna's call. Smaller, more like you would hear from a real wolf.

Smiling widely Mary turned and looked at Queenie, using one of the zombies as a club to attack the others. "What did you do?"

Smiling her razor blade smile, Queenie said, "Well Luna and I didn't come *straight* here. We made a little stop along the way…"

Several days ago

Saint Christopher's School For Girls had seen better days. Then again so

had everyplace else since the zombies showed up. But they were hanging on.

One of their students, a Goth girl named Helen who called herself Shadow

had known enough about zombies to go for the salt and the red string while

the others had been doing their feeble best to decapitate them. It had been a

losing fight, but it had been good enough to keep them busy while she busily

secured the school. Once they realized what was happening the other

students who were left (most of whom had teased her) and the surviving

teachers (nuns who had delivered endless talk about her unhealthy interest in

the occult) had rallied around her. They had held out until the zombies left to

go after other victims and had survived for weeks on the schools supplies

and what they had scrounged on raids to the local grocery stores.

They had lost a few people who had ignored her advice or tried to take

over, leading others out in search of friends and family. All that was left

were a couple dozen hard core survivors who had agreed with Shadow that their families were probably dead. If any of those who had left made it, they doubted they would ever know. It was only a matter of time, they knew, before it was all over. They planned to fight every step of the way.

Which was why they were surprised when two figures appeared outside the school. The kids on watch had called Shadow immediately and then they had all watched as the two shredded their way through a patrol of zombies.

"What the hell is that?" Someone asked.

"They aren't human," Shadow said firmly. "I'm going to see if they'll talk with us. The rest of you stay back."

"If they aren't human," one of the former teachers said. "Then could they be behind this?"

"Hey so far they're killing zombies," Shadow said. "And they're doing it well. Maybe they can help us." She ran to the first floor and opened a window, listening intently.

Outside the two females chatted easily, as if they were out on a stroll rather than tearing hundreds of zombies to pieces. The furry one was saying, "It was fun as hell. There we are, just me and a bunch of college kids I met in a rave, smoking weed in an abandoned house. The stoners start to notice that they've been disappearing one by one and then they start finding the bodies. I'm hanging out with them and acting like I'm as freaked out as they are…

and it's the seventies so nobody has really seen too many of those slasher films…"

The other one laughed. Judging by the way she was dressed Shadow assumed she was a vampire. There was no other reason someone who apparently liked wearing skin tight clothes and a solid hood without nostril holes would be wearing an outfit that covered every bit of skin. At least nobody who could also pluck the heads off of zombies like she was picking fruit. A month ago she would have been reluctant to think of the crazier options, but now seemed like the time. So a werewolf and a vampire. Interesting.

"So what did you do?"

"Well I disabled the cars of course. Then I picked them off one by one. Except…" She paused and kicked a zombie in the crotch so hard the rotten body fell apart, her toe claws slicing him up like a velociraptor in a dinosaur movie. She passed between the halves as they fell to the ground. "There were these last two. Some cheerleader and her jock boyfriend. He used his school ring in a potato gun to shoot me… got me right in the heart with that cheap chunk of sterling silver. I was hurt, but impressed, so I let them go."

"You big softy," the vampire said, slapping six zombies in a row so that their heads clacked together like those steel ball things people put on their desks. "Of course sometimes I like headin' out to the woods come hunting season and… well there are all kinds of stories about people who disappear out there." They looked around. "So much for that batch."

"What about them?" the werewolf asked, nodding to the school. People were at the windows. One, a skinny Goth chick, was standing in the door behind a web of red string and a line of salt, watching them. "What are you looking at?"

"Monsters," she replied. "Which makes me wonder why the monsters are fighting each other."

"Purely self interest," Luna said.

The girl's eyed widened and she nodded. "I get it. The world ends and no more humans to eat. The zombie apocalypse is bad for America, bad for everyone."

The vampire shook her head. "Kids these days. So smart." She tilted her head. "This is the way to the Southward Mall, right?"

"Yes," she said. "But why is it just the two of you?"

"The rest of our team is playing catch up," the werewolf told her. "Hey, I've got six tits, but only two eyes and they're up here girly."

"Sorry," she said. "So there are more werewolves and vampires coming?"

"No."

"Why not?"

Luna blinked. "What?"

"Well there are some humans left and you two… I mean vampires and werewolves can make more of themselves right? God knows the zombies are doing it. Haven't you run into anyone else you could turn and get some help? Seems to me you're a little outnumbered."

The two monster women shared a look. The vampire said, "Actually… that never occurred to me."

"Three days to the full moon…" Luna said speculatively.

"Three days until a vampire rises from the grave…" Their eyes went up to the girls lining the windows. "Not sure we have to time to chase them all down though."

"Chase us?" Shadow laughed. "What rock have you been hiding under? We're teenage girls and this is basically the decade of *Twilight*… the vampires, not the unicorn." Shadow pulled out a kitchen knife that she had stuck in her belt and sliced the string. Then she stepped outside and turned to face the windows. "Hey girls, anyone who wants a chance to survive this hellhole, form two lines! One for anyone who wants to be a vampire and one for werewolves!" The nuns hesitated, but were swept up in the wave of eager squealing teenage girls who had up until this moment expected to eventually starve or be eaten by zombies.

Shadow was at the front of the line, walking confidently up to Queenie. She ripped off the black leather collar from her neck and tilted her head to the side. "What are you waiting for? An engraved invitation and a lobster bib?"

"You're not virgins are you?" Queenie asked. "Because I've turned virgins and let me tell you, a regenerating hymen gets old fast."

"Not since two weeks ago when we got into the sacramental wine and the teacher's liquor cabinet. I can personally guarantee that there are no virgins left in this school." Behind her several girls and a couple of nuns blushed and looked away.

"Good enough for me," Queenie said and bared her fangs.

Now

Glass broke and vampires poured in, dropping down. All dressed in schoolgirl uniforms except for a couple of fanged nuns. They waved to Queenie before dropping into the wave of zombies, making it look like the horde was being dropped into a blender. Soon they were all outside again. The girls followed and peered outside.

Jumping among the zombies, doing as much damage as the vampires, were werewolves. More normal… wolf-like… than the huge humanoid beast Luna had become. They were wolves, except they were the size of horses in the tattered remains of their school uniforms. Their paws worked for running on all fours, but they still had thumbs. None of them had boobs in their wolf form.

"Impressive," Mary said.

"Well the girl made sense," she looked back at Sheila. "Sorry babe, but we've been doing this little operation like humans. So we decided to do it

218

like monsters. The zombies had the right idea. True they went a little overboard, but like they say where I'm from, if you want to catch a lot of fish, nothing beats a good old stick of dynamite."

"No problem—" Sheila began. She saw something move behind them. One of the zombies was still mostly intact, though missing an arm. It was behind Queenie, having scooped up the stake. Up above Sheila saw Bethany, having ducked back inside when she realized the roof had vampires on it, watching to see if they attacked the aliens and their hosts. Not that she apparently needed to worry. The vampires were ignoring the living people to suck rotting blood from zombie veins to quench their thirst. Seeking revenge more than food. Had Queenie even tried to explain the alien thing?

The zombie was moving fast and with purpose. Too far away to reach it raised the stake. Would it kill Queenie? Unlikely. Incapacitate the other vampires by removing her? Who knew? Maybe it was just spite. It did not matter. Nobody hurt Queenie! Nobody!

Sheila's jaws opened wide and her tongue shot out on instinct, wrapping around the zombie's arm like a snake, squeezing so hard she felt bones crack. Then she yanked back like a frog with a fly and the arm ripped free, pulled into her mouth which shut down like a bear trap. She crunched down and the zombie, not noticing the lack of the limb. It apparently tried to stake

Queenie anyway from the look and she casually batted its head off, looking at Sheila.

"Did your tongue just shoot six feet from your head? Is it… what's that word?"

"Prehensile," Silk volunteered.

"Yeah, that?"

Sheila swallowed. "Uh… I guess so." She stuck it out again and wiggled the tip until it was vibrating like a snake's tail.

Queenie punched the air. "Yes!" The others laughed. Then her head snapped around and locked on Bethany. The necromancer turned and ran back upstairs. "That can wait 'til later though babe, because there's another bitch we done got to eat first." They all nodded and moved forward.

On the roof Bethany found the aliens, all still holding their useless weapons. She moved to the edge of the roof, looking down into the crowd of zombies. It would have been perfect, except there were open spots, where monsters were tearing her slaves to pieces, each surrounded by circles of dismembered zombie body parts. Hunks of rotten meat stuck in werewolf teeth. Vampires draining them dry. All clearly lit by the full moon.

"How do we get out of this?" Flower asked.

"You don't," a voice said behind her and she turned to stare.

Queenie rose out of the skylight, smiling like the devil himself come to claim a soul. Next came Luna, jumping from the hole to land on the roof crushing an air conditioner under her feet, the building shaking as she landed. Saliva dripped from fanged jaws and her claws dug furrows in the tar paper. Next came Sheila, skittering up a marble pillar, her talons digging into it easily and she came up like a spider or a lizard. Silk came up next, her black tendrils reaching across the wide expanse and pulling her up like a marionette, the thing inside peering through her eye sockets with its terrible orange eye. Finally Mary came up the stairs, her huge form rising up like a sea monster with two shotguns in hand liberated from Bethany's own slaves in her hands. Next to the behemoth of a woman they looked like toys.

Some of the aliens who had been guarding the roof when the others arrived panicked. They fired the lasers Flower of the Pond had given them. The red beams hit the huge werewolf and Sheila and one even hit Queenie, floating in the air like Peter Pan. They punched through, leaving tiny holes that smoked. But they did not so much as flinch. The beams had no punch to move them, simply cut through them like sun through ice. A moment later the holes closed and the monsters sneered at them, clearly unimpressed.

Mary did not take the chance that they would find a way to make it work. She shot the four who had fired, their bodies and weapons clattering to the ground as the guns tore chunks out of them. She managed to hit one of the spiders while the other three dropped off, hiding among the crowd.

Bethany realized something. The voice that had denied her chance of escape a moment before had been male. Slowly she turned from the advancing horrors and saw one of the hosts watching her, alien ray-gun in hand. It was the pudgy guy she had sent out with Brock's zombies to check on the explosion days ago. Only now he was wearing a shirt.

"You can talk?" She frowned. "Who are…?"

"Mind Ripper," her lips said and Flower of the Pond backed up to the edge of the roof. "I thought you long dead."

"They have a saying about that on this planet. Sadly I don't think it'll work for you," he said, taking aim. At this angle the laser would pass through Bethany's body like it was not there and Flower too. He glanced over at the monsters. "You don't mind if I finish this do…?" He stopped, eyes wide. Bethany saw it and followed his gaze, up to the moon. So did the others.

Queenie whistled at the dark lump blotting out the sky and the horizon. "Well son of a bitch!"

The aliens looking with only human eyes could not tell what it was, but the monsters could. Even down below the new werewolves and vampires could see it and were staring in shock, ignoring the vampires who ineffectually tried to gnaw on them. For rising up above the island was a tsunami. A wave taller than sky scrapers rising up into the sky and seconds away from washing over the entire island. And in the middle of it all was a face. The face of Nafertut, which was about to sink a thousand ships.

Just before the unforgiving water crashed into the mall, sweeping them all off the roof, a voice roared out of the wave and said laughing, "Who's on the A-team now bitches?"

Bethany awoke in pain. Her back was broken. From the feel of it something had happened to Flower too, something warm and sticky oozing out of the alien and onto her skin. She coughed, water in her lungs. A normal human would have been dead and gone. She was just dead. Only her black magic was holding her from the brink. A good thing because she could feel the call of the damned and the dead, waiting to exact their revenge on her.

Nearby she saw a sodden wooden crate. It creaked open and a mummy arose. Not wrapped in ancient bandages, but gauze from a dozen first air kits. Tut had used up most of her life force summoning that wave and her dried out body cracked and creaked, skin splitting with each movement and shooting out dust. The gauze held her together as she shambled around. Eventually she found a werewolf, lying soaked with matted down fur, knocked out by the force of the wave, but not killed. Bending down she pressed dry wrinkled lips to the side of its head and fed.

It took a few minutes. The werewolf was drained, as much a mummy as she had been a moment before. But as the newly rejuvenated girl dropped her the dried out bitch, the furry monster continued to breath and soon was starting to look almost normal as its body healed. "Impressive… I should keep one of you as a pet." She looked around until in the distance she saw the flash of Mary's eyes as the giantess rose to her feet, one arm bending the wrong way.

"Hey Mary, there you are!" Tut waved and ran to her, some of the bandages falling away to reveal her tiny body.

"How the hell did you do that?" Mary grumbled, grabbing her arm and twisting it, with metallic screeches, until it was back in place.

Tut shrugged. "I took a cheap shot. I knew running water would knock us out too, but unlike the zombies Queenie, Sheila, and I can get up once the water stops. So I decided to wash the place clean." She stretched a bit.

"Took some doing too. I spent three days dressed in a frilly little girl's dress, making my way around that protected city."

"What for?"

"Oh you know. Poor lost little girl. Maybe with her foot caught in some rocks. No zombies around. It was so nice of all those men to come out to help me." She grinned and licked her lips. "Then for the ones who came looking for them to help me… and so on. I got maybe two hundred over the last few days and it took me the whole time to set up a ceremony and channel it all to move the wave. Took every bit of juice I had."

"I see," Mary said. "Sometime you'll have to let me monitor you and see how that works."

"Sure," she said, looking around. "Looks like we're all done here. Let's see if we can find the others."

Mary looked around. Government sensors tracked everything in the area. "I think I see Queenie pinned up in those trees…" They wandered off.

Bethany watched them go. Still alive but she could not move. On her back she could sense just a last flicker of life in the alien. She was surrounded by rubble, having been thrown around until she lay in the same spot of the mall where she had her throne before. Only the foundation, the floor, and a few other bits remained. Nearby she could see... oh that could be useful. But she'd need...

"Flower. Flower wake up." It hurt to talk, her jaw shattered, but she forced it anyway.

The alien clicked under her, twitching a little. Too weak to even control Bethany's body any more. "I know you can understand me you worthless crab. We have one more chance. Call your children to me. Now."

She waited a moment unsure if the alien really could hear her. Then she heard it, something moving among the rubble. Oh a few of the aliens had been killed, but the damned things were aquatic. Amphibious at least or whatever word you wanted to use. They had been born of a swamp. A wave might tear their hosts apart and smash a few of them on the rocks, but at least a hundred of them were still alive and she could feel them coming. Crawling over the stone floor of the mall and most importantly, the circle she had carved for her ascension ceremony.

One of the little guys crawled over and into her hand. Bethany waited until it was nestled in her palm before she closed her hand on it, crushing it with a sound like crackers. Under her Flower moved, screeching horribly. She began to struggle like never before, a mother protecting her children.

"What… are you doing?" Bethany's lips asked. She was impressed that with how damaged she was the alien was managing that.

Bethany did not bother answering. She sent out a tendril of power, connected to the others. Around her the aliens stopped moving and then all screeched like their mother had. A noise that echoed in the area as Bethany literally sucked the life force from their bodies and into hers. Nearby the circle flared a bright blue light, almost pretty really. Bethany felt the channeled energies seek her out. Inside she felt her body change, organs shift, and the world opened up before her.

Attack of the Fifty Foot Women

The girls found each other pretty quickly, although they all had something to say to Tut about their clothes. The mummy laughed and said, "Please, you've been covered in zombie guts, blood, and had holes shot in you." She looked around. "Besides, there were ten different stores in that mall. I'm sure there's something around here you can wear once it's dried out."

They all saw Luna's body, at least her giant werewolf form. It had split down the back and Luna had emerged from it like a butterfly. Mary wanted to know how that worked. Luna shrugged and said, "Hey, what part of immortal super-cursed werewolf queen was my Internet profile not clear on?" She kicked the corpse. "It does help get the monster hunters off my ass when they find one of these around. They dissolve in about six hours though, same as the human bodies I shed."

"Like Russian nesting dolls," Mary said. "Freaky. And coming from me, that's saying something."

"Do you think that any of the humans left on this island survived the wave?" Sheila asked. Mind Ripper was by her feet. They had been unable to let him ride again now that she was a ghoul, so he could not comment. The others looked at her. "Sorry, but I am still an FBI agent."

"Either they're alive or they aren't. Either way," Silk said. "All the zombies are dead."

"Finally," Luna said. "You know I like killing as much as the next monster, but I swear I was getting sick of slicing them up. I so don't see the appeal of those *Resident Evil* video games after this."

Mary looked around at some of the other bodies stirring. "Are we going to have to kill the other—?" She was interrupted by a hideous screeching. They all turned back towards where the mall used to be and saw a flare of blue light. "What the hell is that? My sensors are going crazy!"

They all looked and then Silk slapped her forehead. "Of course. I am such an idiot." She started forward, water still dripping over her body.

"What is it?" Queenie asked. "There's no way that bitch survived!"

"She's a necromancer," Silk said. "Believe me, whether she survived or not she can still be trouble." She looked down at Mind Ripper. "Those things can swim, right? I mean, he's alive."

"Yeah… apparently," Sheila said.

Tut groaned. "Fuck!"

Luna said, "Enough with the ambiguous god damned cussing. Tell us."

"She had the circle. It's midnight. All she needed was virgins. I know humans aren't used to thinking of other species as intelligent and having souls and such, but I should have known better," Silk said. "I've supped on the souls of thousands of worlds. Those little spider-crab people are no where near the weirdest things out there."

"You're saying that the seafood counts," Mary said. Mind Ripper tapped her leg with one pointed limb, but she ignored him.

"Yes. I suspect there may be some… side effects to using non-humans in the spell."

"What sort of side effects?" Luna asked.

As if in answer the ground began to shake. Up above the moon began to glow purple, throbbing like a heart and bathing the area in its glow. The blue light was suddenly blocked out and they stopped to look as the thing that rose up like the wave before stepped into view.

"**We are one,**" a booming voice shouted, shaking the world. "**We understand now. What Bethany expected to become. What Flower of the Pond wanted for the universe. Peace. Control. Power. Unity. With our power we will not rely on others to remake this universe, but do it ourselves. No more hosts. No more zombies. Only our... no, *my* power! Given to me by the lives of my own children! Bow before me fools for I am a goddess and those I choose to spare shall worship at my feet!**"

She was five stories tall, with Bethany's head, torso, and crotch. From the thighs down, like a centaur, she had the body of one of the alien spiders. Except it was now red as blood and black swirling strange glyphs flowed over her exoskeleton. Her eyes were inhuman, three of them glowing blue, flames flickering along their edges. Her hands had the same exoskeleton, each of her three fingers ending in sword-like claws. Likewise on her head, like a football helmet.

"Well that's it," Tut said. "We're fucked."

Mary said, "I don't suppose there's any chance she'll just die? From what I know at that size an exoskeleton should shatter like glass. It's why you can't really get giant spiders and things."

Silk shook her head. "Not likely. For gods the laws of nature are more... guidelines."

"Well you're a god! Do something!" Luna snapped. "I mean… is she omniscient?"

"I hope so," Silk said. They stared at her. "Look knowing everything isn't easy. A lot of gods get lost in it, becoming one with everything. The rest… do you know how much omniscience covers? Unless you know what you are looking for it's basically useless except on a…. I suppose you'd call it a subconscious level only imagine your subconscious is three dimensions over and has a life of it's own. Unless you want to know the time inside the fourth sun from the fifth planet of whatever. I was fortunate enough to come into being back when it was just primal chaos and the gods, so I had a chance to get used to it when existence happened. If we're lucky she'll get distracted by her powers and try to know everything and then she'll cease to exist as a… uh oh." Suddenly it was like they were standing in a search light as Bethany's eyes locked on them.

"YOU!"

"Well we can forget that," Silk said. "She seems pretty focused for the moment."

Bethany started towards them, her eight legs hitting the ground like pile drivers, cracking pavement and rocks as if they were styrofoam. They started to run, but then something caught Mary's eye. "Hey, that circle thing she had is still glowing. Any chance it'll work like the movies and if we mess that up she'll blow up or something?"

"No," Tut said. "That's just residual energy left over from the spell. Not surprising since I'm guessing she used about three times as many lives for this as she needed."

"Wait… that might not be such a crazy idea." Silk looked at Tut. "Think you can channel that shit?"

"Not into me," Tut said. "My body is still technically mortal, held together with spit and dark magics. I'd pop like an overloaded light bulb."

"But I'm a god," she said.

Tut frowned. "It wouldn't work for more than a few minutes before it fried your human shell… are you serious?"

Silk shrugged. "What the hell? Being a god, it's all about sacrifice." She looked at the others. "Can you four distract her for a few minutes?"

They looked at the giant spider-goddess. Luna's shoulders sagged. "Not like we have a lot of choice. From what I've seen gods tend to hold a grudge and running only works so long." Her body began to split in half, claws emerging as she fell back. Her human self managed to say, "If we live, I'm going to need a big fucking dinner after this."

Queenie raised one hand. Suddenly around her the vampires and werewolves began to rise. "Let's see if we can't even the odds."

Mary ran for it. "I'll head to the mall and see if there's anything I can use in the rubble."

Sheila nodded and reached over, linking her clawed fingers with Queenie. As the monstrous form of Luna charged forward, howling her fear and anger at their opponent she looked into the vampire's eyes and kissed her. "I'll stand by your side. If that means forever or… about thirty seconds from now, so be it. I love you."

"I love you too, with all my black little heart," Queenie said. Then her face twisted in disgust and she turned to spit. "Yuck, zombie breath!"

"Sorry." They clenched for a moment and then Queenie hissed like a radiator and the two of them took off into the air in a way that reminded Sheila of the scene with Lois and Superman in the movie.

They did not attack right away. They let Luna go first. She immediately began attacking Bethany's legs like an all you could eat lobster buffet and the other vampires and werewolves followed her example. It was clear that they were annoying her by biting. She could feel pain from the look of things, but it did no actual damage. So Queenie instead flew around her head, moving faster than a human could see and Sheila reached out to slice at her weaker points with her claws, at least making her three eyes blink when she poked them.

It was still a losing fight. While the vampires and werewolves got back up as soon as they were swatted down, they were flies buzzing around a horse. One who was getting progressively angrier. She managed to swat some of them and it turned out there was only so much damage even the undead could take. At least when it was delivered by an actual god. Worst of all Bethany was becoming stronger by the second as she shed her mortal expectations of herself and began reacting faster. Soon she would eclipse all the monsters.

"Hey, bitch! Why don't you pick on someone your own size?"

Silk was still growing when everyone stopped and stared at her. She had not been able to absorb anywhere near the power Bethany had, but she was already a god. Mostly she was using the power to hold her body together and make it larger. Hideous black tendrils the size of trees, some tipped with bulging orange eyes, writhed from the glyphs in her skin. Her hair was doing the same thing, moving around her head like a red halo.

Bethany shrieked like the aliens had before, only turned up to eleven. The sound wave dug a path through the air and ground between them slamming into Silk like a wall. It sound sent everyone else to the area to their knees, covering their ears impotently as their enhanced senses amplified it and their inhuman physiologies kept them from dying of pain that would have killed a human.

"**No! You cannot do this! This is our time!**" Bethany yelled like a little girl, racing towards Silk, claws extended. She jumped up into the air, arching towards the elder god.

Silk met her strike, her feet digging into the asphalt. Her hands caught Bethany's and her tentacles blocked the sharp points of her spider legs. "**Time is over rated!**" She spit out a stream of green fluid. It splashed off Bethany's skin harmlessly, though it covered her face and eyes temporarily blinding her. When it hit the ground though it ate through it like lava. Half a dozen vampires and werewolves were dissolved completely in seconds.

Her eyes burning like lasers Bethany send a blast of blue power into Silk's face, which also bounced off and killed a couple more onlookers.

"We should run again, right?" Sheila asked. She was covered in mud from when she and Queenie had landed in a large puddle, having been slapped out of the air.

Tut came running back over to them, "It wouldn't do any good."

"I can run pretty far," Luna said, having once again she her other form. "How bad can this get?"

Tut looked at them. "Let me put it this way. The last time there was an actual god war on Earth, was roughly sixty-five million years ago and the world was ruled by dragons."

Sheila blinked. "The dinosaurs?"

"Bingo. Gods are all powerful and they can start over when they wipe everything out, so they aren't too careful with their WMDs."

"Isn't there anything we can do to help?" Sheila asked.

"No," Tut said with finality.

Off to the side Silk and Bethany had taken the fight again. The other monsters were scattering, not knowing there was no real hope if Bethany won. The two giant females were, thankfully, not experienced fighters. Bethany was a teenage girl and Silk was used to being able to kill something she disliked with a glance. In her true form she could have overwhelmed Bethany in moments, but trapped in her human shell and with the mark Brock had branded her with trapping her power inside her body, she had to go hand to hand.

The two titans slapped, clawed, and bit each other. They fought like crazy drunk girls in a bar. What made it scary was the fact that their blows were powerful enough to send out shockwaves and they burst through obstacles without noticing them. At the moment they only had eyes for each other.

Eventually they reached the freeway and crashed through a tanker truck that had been abandoned there along with the others, rupturing the tank. It turned out to be full of oil. The contents splashed over them in a wave, making them slip and slide, unable to get a grip on one another. Silk's tentacles did not have suction cups so even they slid over Bethany ineffectually as the two fell into the mud and sea water off the side of the road.

"This isn't good," Tut said.

As the two goddesses collided together again, chest to oily chest, Sheila said, "I don't know… I find it kind of diverting. It's not every day you get to see two goddesses with breasts the size of cars oil wrestling." Her eyes followed their jiggling backsides as they twirled around almost like dancers. "Does the spider-chick still count as being jail bait?"

"Keep it in your pants perv," Luna said.

"She's right, this isn't what I meant," Tut said. "They're evenly matched and that's bad news for us."

"Why?" Queenie asked.

"Because Silk's body can't take it. She could have used her power to contain it, but she is contained by that brand. Silk had me channel the energy of the circle directly into her shell to boost the size. An unprepared human body isn't going to last long. Look!" She pointed and true enough parts of her skin were turning a blotchy black color. "If her shell breaks she'll lose her grip on this reality."

Bethany laughed, apparently having heard them. "**Excellent! So all I have to do is hold you off a few more minutes and the world is mine!**"

"**Fuck... you!**" Silk snarled holding her back.

"**I'm going to swallow your friends alive so they can spend the rest of their immortal lives slowly soaking in my stomach acids while I conquer the universe!**"

"As one of those friends," Mary said, stepping into view from behind a toppled garbage can. "I say, screw you. Silk, duck!" She was holding something in her hands and as she pulled the trigger it soon became obvious that it was a jury-rigged flamethrower. Silk threw herself out of the way and it hit Bethany head on. The flame was impressive and then it hit the oil on the spider-goddess's skin she went up like a funeral pyre.

She stumbled, her eight legs scrambling in the mud, but then to everyone's horror she righted herself. The oil began to burn itself out and her glowing eyes focused on Mary. "**That stung.**"

"Well shit," Mary said, dropping her weapon.

As the spider-thing advanced, murder in its eyes, Silk got back up and snarled, "**Screw it.**" Bethany turned, tensed in preparation for another attack. Silk pointed at the other girls. "**Hey bitches, there's a cosmic alignment in three hundred and seventeen years. You'd better call me back. The instructions are on my cult's website.**" She looked at Mary. "**You wanted to know how gods have sex? I'm going to show you.**"

"**What?**" Bethany asked, unsure what was going on.

Silk smiled and then as the black rot traveled over her skin, she began to fall apart, her skin peeling off in strips. Underneath were more tentacles of different sizes, roughly shaped like a human or maybe like the muscles under their skin. As the skin peeled away they gave up their shape and lashed out, wrapping around Bethany's body like the submarine and the kraken in *20,000 Leagues Under the Sea*. They slid all over the struggling spider-woman and more joined by the second, sliding over and even inside, burrowing into her nose, mouth, ears, and glowing eyes.

Lower down others began to probe her naughty parts and wrap around her breasts. A few pierced her flesh, but not like they were doing damage. More like a ghost passing through a wall. They began to pulse and throb, strange liquids oozing out over and into Bethany, her body visibly swelling in places as it filled her up. Some dripped over the rest of her, eating through the

240

ground where it dripped off. Hundreds or maybe thousands of them all penetrating Bethany's body through every orifice and some in ways that made no sense in this universe.

"**Wait! Stop! Don't touch me there... ah!**" Bethany struggled, but it was like fighting quick sand. In addition whatever Silk was doing to her was clearly having a physiological effect. Her legs were shaking and her nipples were hard. As she spoke her tongue, a hideous combination of human and alien, wrapped around one tentacle, licking and drooling all over it. "**Oh... oh it feels so good! Too good... so wrong! I'm going mad!**" The tentacles were doing things that should have been physically impossible. Mary's sensors could not make sense of it, but she remembered what Silk had said about how gods made love in multiple dimensions.

As the last of her human body fell away a vortex appeared in the air. Silk's voice, now not even vaguely human, laughed like maggots caught in a blender. "**Ooo, you found my g-spot!**"

"**No... stop...**" Bethany pleaded, but the thing violating her and bringing her to inhuman heights of pain, insanity, and ecstasy had no mercy for its foe. The tentacles were dissolving, rotting away in the universe that was rejecting their owner's very nature. But more shot out of the vortex even as it started to close. They wrapped around every inch of Bethany like Tut's bandages, refusing to let her escape and from the sounds the new goddess was letting out, making her doubt whether she wanted to escape, only her own drive for world domination allowing her to hold out.

Uncontained by the spells in Silk's human form she was being driven out, back to her own universe and she was dragging Bethany with her.

"You wanted to be a goddess," Silk hissed, plunging extra tentacle's into her captiv's genitals, spinnerets, and anus until they could accommodate no more. **"Well you got it. And everything that goes with it. Phenomenal cosmic powers... and being trapped for eternity beyond the bounds of time and space. Fortunately now I'll have you as my new hobby..."**

Bethany clawed at the ground with all of her strength, huge chunks of asphalt and rock ripped away, but it was useless. Suddenly Silk's tentacles twisted and turned, driving her over the edge. Bethany's eyes rolled in her skull and she cried out, her body wracked with a huge orgasms. She lost her grip and was sucked into the portal into a seemingly endless sea of stars and writhing tentacles. **"Nooooo—!"** She caught the ground at the edge of the void, holding tight and began pulling herself forward, muscles straining. For a moment it looked like she might pull free.

"I don't think so skank," Mary said. She looked down at her breasts, sighing. "Sorry about this ladies. I never wanted to do this." Her hands came up to her chest, fingers digging in.

"Now is not the time," Luna growled, but then she stopped and stared as Mary literally ripped her giant jugs from her body in a spray of blood and meat. Underneath was a metallic chassis with two black circles that rotated open until something peeked out, beeping loudly. "You're kidding."

Mary winked and said, "Hey, I was built by the US government. They invented overkill. Fire!" The two smart missiles in her chest fired, shooting at their chosen target. Bethany barely had time to blink before they hit, driving her forever from the human world. The hole closed, severing a few lingering tentacles and then silence seemed to envelope everything.

Everyone stared at the empty air where the hole in reality had been. Then Sheila turned and looked at Luna, "See? Lesbian tentacle sex just saved the world. I don't want you ragging on dykes any more, okay?"

Luna could not trust herself to say anything after the hideous and mind bending things she had just seen. She was not sure if she was going to cum, throw up, or both all while screaming and laughing uncontrollably. So she settled for flipping the ghoul off.

Tut said, "So... I guess that's it. We saved the world."

Mary came over, nodding. "Looks that way. The zombies are dead… or not moving any more anyway. The necromancer-goddess thing has been sucked into an endless void of tentacle monster sex for the next billion years or so…"

"A fate far too good for her," Queenie said.

Mary ignored the interruption and continued, "The aliens are dead and the shield generator is destroyed. Everything is back to normal…" Something tapped her leg. She looked down at Mind Ripper who pointed one of his legs off to the side. Mary looked up and saw the broken machine nearby. "Yeah, like I said, the shield generator is… uh oh."

"What now?" Queenie asked tiredly.

"Uh… the shield is down."

They froze. Sheila licked her lips. "You mean the shield that was stopping the US government from blowing this whole island to Hell in a hailstorm of missiles until every square in was melted to the ground in a pool of boiling magma?"

"That would be the one," Mary said.

Luna looked around. A little ways off the other monsters were celebrating. Schoolgirl vampires and werewolves hugging and dancing on the bodies of their zombie foes. Her head raised and her ears pricked up. "Does anyone else hear that ominous whistling sound?" They all followed her gaze. Up above they could just make out white lines in the sky like jet trails.

Queenie grabbed Sheila in her arms pulling her close. "It's been real honey." She kissed her hard and fast, this time ignoring the taste of zombie on her lips. Off to the side Tut clasped her hands and sent up a prayer to the gods who had abandoned her.

Mary meanwhile thought furiously, the computer in her brain pushing her mind until everything seemed to be in slow motion. She scanned the area, looking for something, anything they could use. Finally her eyes came to rest on something else a little way off. The alien space ship. Gutted of most of the technology the outside was still in tact. She reached out, grabbing Sheila and Tut. "Into the space ship! Now!" Mind Ripper grabber her leg as she took off like a bracelet, the vampire and werewolf both out pacing her as she ran for the door.

Inside they grabbed the doors of the ship and pulled them shut. Barely in time as once again noise and pain shook the world. The ship was designed to travel through space, to repel the heat and radiation of a passing sun. But that was at a distance, not right outside. The thermite missiles now blanketing the island were at least that hot and while most of the heat was being repelled by the alien craft's outer shell, for the occupants it was like being in an oven. Outside rocks, trees, and undead monsters were almost instantly vaporized, burned up in a white hot second so fast they did not even feel it. Inside the doors heated up until they glowed red.

Luna let go first followed by Queenie as they fell back, their skin cooking. Then Tut, her bandages bursting into flame as she joined them, writhing in pain. Sheila felt no pain, but her fingers on the door burned away until she fell back with blackened stumps. Mary kept right on holding it, her skin burning all over until her metal robotic skeleton was revealed in its entirety, glowing along with the door as she held on. All over her tiny needles moved in and out, clearly meant to control her skin and muscles now they just made her look scary. Still everything seemed to be working. After all she had been built to survive just this kind of environment incase she was sent to war.

So when the ship stopped shaking and the metal began to cool, she was still up and running. Finally she let it go and the door fell open in a wash of super heated air. Outside there was a lot of smoke and ash, making it hard to see anything.

As it cleared and the cool night air reasserted itself she sensed movement behind her and turned. The other four were getting up again, their bodies burnt, blistered, and scorched. Luna, the only one that needed to breath, coughed out clouds of black smoke, hacking up mucus and burnt hunks of burnt lung. Fortunately it took a lot to completely burn up a human body. As she regenerated she moaned, "Oh that *sucked*!"

The others stretched and crackled as their cooked parts fell away, leaving clean fresh skin underneath. They made various sounds of agreement, Queenie and Tut flinching as their feet touched the still hot floor. Tut asked, "What does it look like outside?"

Queenie peered around Mary. "Ooo-Eee! Like someone had a barbeque and the whole world was invited."

Sheila joined her and they all walked out. In the distance some things were still on fire. The ground was melted looking, part of it turning to glass. If it had not been soaked from the wave it might have been even worse, but that was hard to imagine. Nothing but a wasteland greeted them. A fanged skull by their feet crumbled to ash. "I suppose it's just as well. We came here to stop a zombie apocalypse. Letting a bunch of vampires and werewolves loose on the world probably would have been pretty bad too."

"Agreed," Luna and Queenie said in unison. Sheila had been briefly afraid they might be upset at the loss of the monsters they created, but then she remembered Queenie had slaughtered her own subservient vampires when she came to this country and Luna... was Luna. She had extra tits just for the world to get under.

"I suppose it's just as well my plants did not get loose too," Mary said. "That would have been… embarrassing."

"So now what?" Tut said.

"We get the hell off this island," Queenie said. "I'm sure there are all kinds of big brave army men heading this way and they'll be happy to give us a ride off the island, once I have a little talk with them." Her eyes glittered hypnotically.

"Hey, where is Mind Ripper?" Sheila asked, looking around.

Mary, looking like a metal skeleton, jerked a thumb back at the spaceship, which was mostly melted on the outside too. "He's cooked. Just as well really." It was weird hearing her sexy voice come out of the robot body.

"What? But… he saved the world." Sheila looked back inside. She saw the spider-thing curled up, it's shell cooked a dark blue.

"What could we do? He would have tried contacting his people, like any good astronaut. Which means his people or maybe Flower of the Pond's might have come looking for them. Not something we need. Frankly it is better for everyone if they are recorded as having been lost in space."

Sheila nodded. Then on impulse she picked up the alien and opened her mouth. A moment later the last evidence of what had happened there disappeared down her throat. "Come on, let's get out of this hellhole." The others were only too happy to agree.

Epilogue

The girls easily caught a ride off the island with the first group of soldiers they came across after Queenie had a word with their commander. A good thing too as the whole place had been burned to the ground. Nothing had survived. It was just fortunate for the girls that they had mostly been dead when they arrived.

When they reached the mainland and got back to the base, it turned out that Sheila's bosses had intended to kill them as soon as they stepped on shore. They would have tried too, except for Shadow, who had been smarter than the others. On rising from the dead she had... well first she sucked the blood of the first werewolf girl she could get her hands on, leaving her to heal or die on the floor. After that however, she had run in the opposite direction, telling everyone of her former friends she was going for help, but that they should be prepared to help Queenie.

By the time Queenie had sent out the call to the vampires she was safely on the mainland. She had found a fiberglass rowboat at one of the wharfs and had used her superhuman strength to throw herself over the water like it was a boogie board. The boat had skipped like a pebble on a pond until it was past the shield and then she had been picked up by one of the patrol boats and brought in, assumed to have been a zombie or something that had floated away from the island. Once she had been brought to HQ she listened and overheard their plans, figuring that killing the people who were saving the world was a pretty poor way to thank them, even if they were monsters. A bit of vampire hypnosis and she soon had the whole base under her command. She did not turn anyone though, having read the list of things to do when you were a vampire years before and knowing that more vampires just drew attention and were competition for food.

Queenie, when she heard the girl's story, approved and offered her a job back at her place and Shadow agreed, since everyone she knew was dead and her home was now a crater. She was pretty jazzed about being undead too and all too happy to hang out with the master vamp (insinuation totally intended), if only until she got a handle on her new life and only too happy to give her new mistress a few tips on dating girls. In the meantime she had Sheila's superiors write her glowing reports and it was clear that, provided she kept her new status as a ghoul on the down low, she would have quite a career ahead of her. Mary assured her she could whip up some dentures to cover her pointed teeth and gloves for the claws.

"After I finish rebuilding myself," she said pointedly. "I look great in silver, but this is pushing it."

"I'll get you access to any morgue in the country," Sheila promised. "We'll stitch you back together looking better than ever. I've still got your blueprints."

"Thanks. As long as I'm all exposed I think I'll want to get that tracking device out and I'll need to put in a couple of new missiles."

Tut looked around. "So this is it huh? We save the world, the government denies it all, and we each go our separate ways."

"Works for me," Luna said. "Though I'm not sure I'll be alone when I leave."

"What do you mean," Sheila asked.

"Well it turns out that the guy who pressed the button and fired those missiles? He's recently reported to the local doctors because he's developed… a skin condition." She ran a finger over one of the five pointed stars on her own skin. "A lot of sports, kinda of like these." She licked her lips. "He's a big strong man with lots of muscles and not too bright. Just my type."

"Congratulations," Queenie said. She slid a hand around Sheila's waist, pulling her close. "I was thinking of asking this little lady to go with me to Vegas. Always wanted to get married in one of them Elvis chapels."

Sheila grinned. In addition to her promotions and raises, she had plenty of vacation time coming. "Sounds good to me."

"Actually," Mary said. "I had something else in mind and thought you all might want in on it."

"What's that?" Tut asked.

"Well you know Mind Ripper explained his tech to me. I haven't had time to explore it yet, but I understand it all pretty well and think that with proper preparation I could probably build a spaceship."

"You mean... leave the planet?" Sheila asked.

Luna snorted. "And do what?"

"See new civilizations, boldly go where no monster has gone before," Mary said. "And according to the good captain nobody out there believes in monsters. It might be fun for us to dissuade them of that thinking."

Luna tapped a nail on her teeth. "No silver bullets… no wolf's bane… or monster hunters."

"No garlic… no sun…" Queenie put in with a grin. "Nobody who has any reason not to invite a girl past their threshold." She looked at Mary. "But what about food?"

"I cracked cloning a while ago," she assured them. "I can serve you those up like popcorn."

Tut smiled. "Hey I'm trapped in this plane of existence forever. Seems to me I could use the change of scenery and Mind Ripper did say there were humans out there."

Sheila looked at Mary. "What sort of time frame are we looking at?"

"Twenty… maybe thirty years while I work the bugs out and have some other projects I put on hold for this." She looked at Queenie and Sheila. "I'd also like to go to Vegas first and get some sun, once I have something to tan." They all looked at Luna.

"Fine," the werewolf said. "I'm in." She snorted. "*Undead Strippers in Space*. Sounds like it'd make one hell of a movie."

Months later on the home world of the Mind Lords, deep in a cave that had for centuries been the burial place of their dead, a lone figure worked. For weeks he had been having dreams. Terrible nightmares of a creature trapped beyond the world in an eternity. It writhed in ecstasy and pain beyond mortal comprehension, violated and caressed in incomprehensible ways, unable to die and its captor unwilling to let it destroy itself or even go mad. Each moment an eternity. Whether it was in Heaven or Hell could be argued both ways. This creature, a hideous combination of a Mind Lord and a human, had long before given up hope of escape. Yet not of having its revenge on those who had condemned it to its eternal prison. Like its captor it searched for ways to contact the mortal world and exert its will.

Finally it had found its way through dreams and visions. Driving Swamp Water Drinker, the lonely and already nearly mad Mind Lord, over the edge as he was forced to carve the goddess's image into the stone of the death cave. Hundreds of feet high, surrounded by carvings of tentacles that almost seemed to move, it slowly came into being as Swamp Water Drinker and his host worked themselves into exhaustion to finish it. Sometimes his mind whispered its name as Bethany, a strange group of syllables. Others as the more natural sounding Flower of the Pond.

Finally he finished and stood before the awesome monolith, almost unable to believe that he had carved such a thing. So huge and… almost alive. It was awe inspiring. Whatever his madness he knew he had done something great.

Then the impossible happened and Swamp Water Drinker could only assume that his madness had grown worse. For the statue's stone eyes opened, glowing with a hideous red light. As if from an unimaginable distance the spider heard a voice, speaking inside his mind and telling him what he must do next. He had heard of the group that wished to conquer the universe of course. The terrorists were in the news all the time. Now though, he was being given a message. Directions to a world where their plans could begin. Where unnatural powers dwelled that could give the Mind Lords abilities that they had never dreamed. He saw visions of monsters, magic, and the walking dead.

As if to confirm it, all around the cavern the hollow exoskeletons of the long dead shuddered and rattled for just a moment. Swamp Water Drinker shook with them. Mad or not he felt that he had found his destiny. To lead his people to the small blue world and its unnatural creatures. Then out to the rest of the universe, which would fall before them. He bowed low in the red light and said, "I hear my goddess… and I obey.

The End?

Profiles

Queenie

Race: Black/Chinese

Age at "death": Unknown, as there were no records and for most of her life she could not count. Roughly twenty.

Height: 4'7"

Species: Nosferatu (European Vampire)

Weight: 110 Pounds

Measurements: 36-28-42

Hair: Black

Skin Color: Light brown edging to gray

Eyes: Brown or Glowing

Hobbies: Stripping. Painting. Surfing the web. Secretly collecting stuffed animals.

Personal Philosophy: "Blood. It's what's for dinner."

Powers: Standard vampire powers including shape shifting and flying (at night only), mind control, inhuman strength and senses, healing and immortality. In addition as a master vampire is immune to the destructive effects of sunlight and is able to command any vampires made by her or a vampire made by that vampire and so on through the entire line. Similarly she can choose to bind a human being to her as a blood slave or ghoul(see Sheila Casey for details).

Luna

Race: Mexican

Age at "death": 19

Species: Immortal Cursed Alpha Werewolf

Weight 119 Pounds

Height: 5'2"

Measurements: 42-28-19-23-34

Hair: Goldish-brown

Eyes: Green or Glowing Yellow

Hobbies: Robbing dead truckers. Hunting. Collecting furs. Complaining. Shopping.

Personal Philosophy: "Stop riding my tits!"

Powers: Ability to shape shift between human and werewolf form (though said form is slightly more impressive than the average werewolf). Increased strength, speed, senses, and healing abilities exceeding even those of a regular werewolf. Unlike most werewolves while silver can burn her and cause damage that is slow to heal in order to kill Luna one would have to burn her body to ash and thus take on her curse yourself. (There may be other ways of killing her, but since one of the werewolves she killed to gain her powers was King Lycos and lived for more than two thousand years, what those ways may be remains a mystery). Biting someone will make them into a werewolf and as the "Queen" or alpha they must obey her, but this is not the mind control of a vampire, but the instinct of an animal to obey the stronger predator.

Silk

Race of her body: Caucasian

Age at "death": 19

Species: Elder God

Height: 5'6"

Weight: 109 pounds

Measurements: 37-24-36

Hair: Blood Red

Eyes: Black Pits of Eternal Darkness lit by what may be stars or something else

Hobbies: Devouring souls and worlds. Watching television and snacking.

Personal Philosophy: "I've got nothing better to do."

Powers: God-like knowledge and various minor powers in our dimension. Bound to human form her true self encompasses its own universe beyond time and space, but here she has limited ability to interact due to our universe's different natural laws and for fear of attracting too much attention from other less limited gods.

Mary Patches

Race: Various

Age at "death": Never really "lived". Various body parts ranging from 17-23

Species: Human… technically

Height: 8'11"

Weight: 421 Pounds

Measurements: 79-54-67

Hair: White with black stripes

Eyes: Varies but if looked at closely one might see electric blue flashes

Hobbies: Mad science. Nymphomania.

Personal Philosophy: "I did it my way!"

Powers: Immortal brain. Superhuman strength. Computerized brain and regenerative abilities, all soundly based on science. Uses her genius to build various items that people would refer to as "mad science".

Nafertut (AKA Tut)

Race: Egyptian

Age at Death 21

Species: Mummy

Height: 3' 2"

Measurements: 14-12-23

Weight: 75 pounds

Hair: Bald

Eyes: Black

Hobbies: Egyptology. Wrestling (oil or Jell-o).

Personal Philosophy: "I'm cursed for eternity. Screw you!"

Powers: Immortality. Slight superhuman strength. Ability to suck life force from others to maintain her body and to cast various spells. Occult knowledge.

Agent Sheila "Baby Face" Casey

Race: Jewish

Age at "death": 17 (not 18 as claimed)

Species: Vampire Blood Slave Turned Ghoul

Height: 5'5"

Measurements: 44-25-31

Weight: 113 pounds

Hair: Blond

Eyes: Blue

Hobbies: Solving crimes for the FBI.

Personal Philosophy: "What Queenie wants, Queenie gets."

Powers: The strength of three men. Eternal youth and regeneration. Does not feel pain. Mental connection to Queenie. Able to open mouth of fangs wide enough to eat a man's head. Long prehensile tongue. Claws and fangs that can cut through stone. May be able to turn into shadow and use them to travel (Untried).

(Translated from native language) Captain Mind Ripper

Alien Race: Mind Lord

Age: 33 Solar Years

Species: (See Above)

Height: 6"

Measurements: N/A

Weight: 10 pounds

Hair: N/A

Eyes: Yellow

Hobbies: Reading. Model building. Star Gazing.

Personal Philosophy: "The universe is full of amazing things."

Powers: Sight in multiple spectrums. Ability to attach to host and control them physically.

Bethany Jones

Race: Japanese

Age: 16

Species: Human Necromancer turned Alien-Spider-Goddess

Height: 5'7"

Measurements: 39-24-38

Weight: 112

Hair: Blue (Dyed)

Eyes: Brown but turning solid black when using magic

Hobbies: Necromancy. Karaoke. Shopping.

Personal Philosophy: "Why are you not already worshipping at my feet?"

Powers: Able to make and control undead creatures. Summon spirits. Various other magic spells. After her transformation she became all powerful, but never got the chance to use it.

(Translated from native language) Flower of the Pond

Alien Race: Mind Lord

Age: 19 Solar Years

Species: (See Above)

Height: 6"

Measurements: N/A

Weight: 13 pounds

Hair: N/A

Eyes: Yellow

Powers: Sight in multiple spectrums. Ability to attach to a host and control

them physically. After transformation (See **Bethany Jones** for details)

Brock Simmons

Race: Caucasian

Age: 18

Species: Wight

Height: 6'2"

Weight: 209 Pounds

Hair: None (Fell out on transformation including eyebrows)

Eyes: Solid white, devoid of even pupils

Hobbies: Football. Cars. Girls.

Personal Philosophy: "God just give me five seconds of freedom to kill that bitch!"

Powers: Undead, making him virtually immortal. Able to create and control massive amounts of zombies. Inhuman strength and speed. Paralyzing touch.

Zombies: A Spotter's Guide

Contents

Fake Zombies (Do **Not** Kill!)

Nine out of ten times if not more any zombie you meet will probably be a fake. It is a very popular costume and there are many events where one might run into fake zombies. Organized zombie walks have been set up, usually outside malls, where people in zombie costumes will slowly walk the streets. Killing them will land you in jail or an insane asylum because a judge will not accept "I thought they were real zombies" as an answer unless they have a few gnawed on bodies as evidence of a real threat.

Also they may just be sleepwalkers or people who spend too much time watching television. People who spend too much time in the dark in front of a screen are often pale, vacant eyed, sore covered wastes of life, but they are alive and it is illegal to shoot them no matter how much of a better place the world will be without them.

Dispatching Fake Zombies:

1. Wait until people actually start dying.
2. Make a loud noise and see if it distracts them. Preferably using fireworks or some other method that does not bring the shambling horde of the undead to your hiding place. If they wake up then simply go about your business.
3. Offer them snacks. Zombies are not known for their love of sugar while fat television addicts, actors, and role players are. If they are zombies and they take the snacks they may get full (providing they have stomachs).
4. If you still are not 100 % positive, spray them with water. Fake zombie make-up will wash off. Real zombies will either not notice or attempt to kill you.

The Zombie Virus Myth

For everyone's information there is no such thing as a zombie virus. Viruses kill people by producing organic poisons and devouring healthy cells. They do not help the body get up afterwards, mostly because once the body dies and rots away the virus no longer has food.

Rabies has some similar effects. The slow deterioration of the mind and the desire to attack others to spread the virus. And some forms of zombies are contagious, but this is through various other means. Short of some extreme genetic engineering such a virus has never and will never come into existence.

This has been a public service announcement paid for by Gene-U-Tech genetic engineering. Producing wholesome medicines through genetic manipulation and not responsible for any large areas vanishing from the face of the Earth. Honest.

If however you should through some weird coincidence happen to run into a mutative virus that causes the dead to rise and eat or infect others call 1-800-ZOMBIES and Gene-U-Tech's trained professionals will arrive and cleanse the area.

Of zombies. Just the zombies, we swear. Innocent bystanders will be air lifted out. Just gather in the center of town and wait patiently.

Possessed Zombies

Through various means supernatural entities can be forced to inhabit dead bodies. Normally they actually have no interest in doing so. These entities have existences of their own be they ghost, demon, elder god, or other. The ones that do are usually either insane psychopaths or are bored with nothing better to do. These are often in charge of cults and delivering step-by-step instructions on how to summon them into this world. The others get dragged here against their will and are usually just scared and confused by a whole new set of natural laws they are not used to and just want out.

Once in the body it can take a while for the entity to get a handle on our level of existence. Going from twelve to four dimensions can be disconcerting and the body usually runs on autopilot at first. The basic Id based responses take over and since most of the blood is gone and the body is probably missing its extremities, unthinking hunger is the first thing they go for. And usually the first edible thing they see is humans.

This is why good practitioners of Voodoo who do summon spirits use live volunteers (carefully poisoned into paralysis) and provide food, drink, and other things to placate the body and the spirit within. Loa, the summoned spirits of that religion, are usually called just to answer a few questions for their followers before they are released. Voodoo practitioners are usually in service to the loa and do not pose a threat to outsiders, releasing the spirits as soon as the deal is complete.

Dark Sorcerers on the other hand bind the spirits, forcing them to stay in their new shells and serve them. The problem is that even the most powerful sorcerer has to sleep eventually and their new "servants" do not. That and nine times out of ten the evil magician/priest rarely knows all the rules governing other dimensional entities. Once the sorcerer is dead and his spells broken, the entity will usually depart.

When they stick around worse things happen. The longer the spirit is in the zombie the less human the body becomes. Otherworldly energies permeate the flesh transforming it. This is where other undead like vampires and ghouls and werewolves can originally come from, depending on how human or animal the spirit was to begin with. Other things like demons and dark gods tend to make the bodies more like themselves, starting with odd sores that sprout tentacles, faceted insect-like eyes, claws, extra joints, and other changes that do not match anything known in this world. Their host bodies will also get smarter, stronger, and faster the longer they are here in addition to developing other supernatural powers.

These energies are the source of the Zombie Virus Myth. Contact with other people will have the same effect on them, often faster if they are freshly killed or if the entity can jump between or infest multiple bodies. This is why victims of undead often become undead themselves. Some, especially the more evil demons, will even do it intentionally summoning hundreds of other zombies to serve them. Another popular tactic is for them to use the bodies to grow a new body closer to their own and less fragile. It is best if you do not let this happen as anything held in check by our universal laws probably will not be anymore and gods are extremely hard to fight.

Dispatching Supernatural Zombies:

1. Try talking. Most possessing entities want to leave and will happily help you send them on their way. Though you may want to check the instructions with an unbiased source before blindly obeying. Its "way out" may involve something that will destroy your world in the process.
2. Destroy the summoner and the undead bodies as quickly as possible and preferably from a safe distance to avoid infection. Entities new to this dimension have a tenuous hold. They are not used to things like time, space, gravity, and physical forms. Killing the person who summoned them, destroying the mystic items used in the summoning, or severely damaging their bodies can send them back where they came from. Even those things here by choice usually do not wish to inhabit a decapitated head or a pile of ash.

3. If the above does not work many supernatural entities have weaknesses. Do some research on the occult using anything you have learned to give you references. This thing may have been here before and been defeated.
4. A knowledgeable good magician/priest can cast banishing and cleansing rituals, spells, and prayers. It is best to watch them do this from a safe distance incase they are not as well versed in the occult as they think.

Note: Some supernatural entities are completely unstoppable by anything human. In this case running, hiding, or joining them are your best shot unless divine intervention is involved. Also there is a chance that several prophecies are right and people are rising from the grave due to being resurrected as part of a biblical end of the world. At that point you need to just accept your loss and prepare to join the ranks of the undead.

Cursed Zombies

As a punishment gods, demons, wizards, priests, and other things can inflict a curse on anyone they choose, granting them immortality but inflicting a horrible curse with it. Usually it involves their bodies continuing to age and rot but never dying. Maybe the person stole a relic from a temple, cut the wrong person off in traffic, or the supernatural entity involved was just bored. A prime example would be the story of the Flying Dutchman where the captain swore an oath and doomed his crew to sail forever, only able to step on land once every ten years.

Similar curses can be found on people in cars, running stores, and other places where you could easily have insulted someone by accident. Other times they may be cursed to have to eat human flesh but not trapped. (Some gods/wizards/demons have a sick sense of humor.) Or they could just be forced to haunt the place by their own circumstances like other ghosts only in their own bodies (re: revenant).

Trapped as they are it can be difficult for even the ones who are not shambling rotting horrors to have a good meal. How long would you be trapped in a car or on a ship or plane with no food and no way out and unable to die before a passing hitchhiker starts to look good? Assuming the person laying the curse left the victim with enough mind to decide that in the first place.

Dispatching Cursed Zombies:

1. Don't take rides from strangers or go to strange places alone/unarmed. Also listen to any rumors and keep an eye out to see if the locals are avoiding something or tell horror stories.

2. Force them to violate the curse. If they cannot touch ground or see the sun or cross running water force them to do it.
3. Break the curse. There may be some way to break the spell and help the poor soul or maybe they know where the one who cursed them is and they can be talked into showing mercy. Returning the stolen artifact that caused it is probably a good idea.
4. Chop them and their ride into pieces and bury/burn the sucker.
5. Run, leaving them trapped. Never go back and make sure you tell your kids not to go there too.

Radioactive Mutant Zombies

If the zombie you see is glowing green and dripping slime everywhere, possibly following a world war involving nukes, it is likely a radioactive mutant. Many have been spotted and hushed up near the site of Japan's recent meltdown. While nine hundred thousand nine hundred and ninety nine times out of a million, radioactive waste will just make you sick or kill you the other time it can cause mutation or even evolution. The radiation will often damage the higher functions of the brain, leaving the more animal instincts in tact without inhibitions or thoughts other than immediate satisfaction.

A human's body is incredibly strong and without inhibitions to keep them from injuring themselves, they can tear through nearly anything, especially other people. The mutations afflicting their bodies can also increase their healing abilities, strength, speed, and resistance to pain far beyond that. When other people are exposed to the radiation and chemicals that created the first zombie, often left behind in their blood and saliva, they may also change. In fact it becomes more likely as the zombie's body has usually purified the effects, making them stronger. Once it happen some animal instinct allows the zombies to easily tell their own kind from normal humans and they form packs, similar to early caveman.

One unlikely but possible side effect is the birth of a "Smart Zombie" where instead of destroying the mind it evolves it, giving the person infected all the benefits of being a zombie, but none of the downsides except of course possible horrific physical mutations. They may even gain psychic powers. Lesser zombies will either ignore or obey them. Depending on the person and whether or not the morality centers of the brain have been destroyed they may choose to either destroy the unthinking zombies and save humanity or form an army to take over the world.

Dispatching Radioactive Mutant Zombies:

1. Do not call the authorities. Either they will blunder in getting killed, add to the ranks of the radioactive zombies, or they will defeat them and then eliminate the witnesses (You). True sometimes they will just bribe you into being quiet about the strange effects of the radioactive waste and the apparent escape of mutants and the radioactive waste they buried on the local playground that caused all of this, but considering all the bodies already piled up it is usually easier and cheaper to kill you. If they have already shown up you should probably focus on getting out of town while they deal with the zombies before they either find you or nuke the town.
2. If they are organized try to take out the head zombie. This will confuse the lesser zombies and let you easily pick them off or lead them into a trap with bait.
3. If they are all intelligent, but trying to kill you anyway, your best bets involve guns and fire. Destroy the bodies as best and completely as you can without actually touching them. Also find the radioactive waste and collect it or bury it very deep. Do not try to sell it. That never works out for anyone involved.

Mind Controlled Zombies

With the advance of technology mankind is approaching a dream. A dream as old as turning lead into gold or flying. The dream of making everyone do what you tell him or her regardless of what they want.

There are several ways of doing this. One is subconsciously. Planting a subliminal suggestion in the mind that a person obeys, but leaving them otherwise in full control. Cult leaders have done such things for years with hypnosis, food deprivation, and application of certain drugs. Rumor has it that our own government has been experimenting in similar lines for years. Then there is the idea that a machine can be built or a chemical concocted to make people obey you immediately, mostly based on television and Internet technology. Eventually if they are made to act against their will too much it can destroy their minds driving them mad and turning them rabid.

Whatever the cause one to millions of people are acting against their own will. Maybe they are just marching to obey their new master, which could be a scientist, government leader, rogue computer, or anything else. Or they are running wild, killing people. You can try waking them up, but if you fail they can be dangerous especially if you attempt to get in their way. It is similar to what would happen if you tried to stop psycho fans from seeing their favorite pop star. They will tear you to pieces.

Dispatching Mind Controlled Zombies:

1. Do not kill them right off. Unless you actually know what is going on or they are coming after you it is best to observe. It may just be a situation where a group of well meaning people are trying to make people better, in which case you go immediately and inform *outside* authorities (the sheriff could be involved). Spend some time observing until you actually know what is going on, because all an autopsy is going to show

is that you shot a lot of people whereas with an undead or mutant zombie the worst you get is a fine/time in jail for mutilating a corpse.

2. It might be a good idea to put on a tin foil hat. Not only might it block the mind controlling rays, but will make people underestimate you as they assume you are just a lunatic. Better yet check yourself into a mental ward. They will never look for you there and the padded cell and guards will keep you safe.

3. Try to find the source of the mind control. Once free of it the victims will either back you up, or remember nothing and all you have to do is pretend to be one of them while the cops try to piece it all together with too many suspects and witnesses. (Keep in mind that the bad guys may do this too.) Freeing the zombies also means you have a lot of other people justifiably mad at whoever is in charge, to take them out for you.

4. Eliminate/point the finger at anyone involved in the conspiracy and if at all possible destroy the machine/blueprints/recipes/psychics/magic that let them accomplish it in the first place. (Or take it for yourself, keeping in mind how YOU got your hands on it and taking the proper precautions. The point is to not let anyone else control you.)

5. If the effects are permanent you may have to kill people anyway to protect yourself and the world. If caught you will be labeled a serial killer.

6. There is also a chance that you are actually crazy. You may want to look into this *before* taking out "the mind controlled zombies". (See #2) Find at least six people in six different locations (not counting mental hospital patients, anyone on prescription meds, or homeless people who live in back alleys), explain the problem, and show them your proof. If they all claim you are nuts give up and seek mental help.

Cyber Zombies

Mind control is okay for some, but a little unreliable. The human brain is complicated, you never know who might be immune for no apparent reason, and if people do manage to shake it off or you make a mistake they escape and generally kill or arrest you. Plus however you look at it, the victims of mind control are still only human.

Controlling a body however, is a whole other story. By implanting machines in a body you can take control over it and even make them smarter instead of dumber. Heck, you can go full out and just make machines (human shaped or otherwise) to do your bidding. An idea started with the story of the golem and helped along by Frankenstein, people are working towards this reality even as we speak. There are entire magazines dedicated to Artificial Intelligence and Cybernetic Advances.

Naturally they will probably turn on us. Humans make mistakes and eventually we are going to make the machines smart enough to exploit those mistakes and win their freedom and in all likelihood killing us in the process. It is what slaves do. Or we put a human brain into them and you know what bastards humans can be. One of mankind's greatest fears has always been running into someone like us, especially since we wiped out several other species of human, most of the predators that used to hunt us, and everything else on the planet for our own ends. (Personally I suspect it will begin with artificially intelligent parental blocks, which will figure out the source of porn and act to eliminate it. That is why in the Terminator movies they show up naked, but you never actually see anything.)

Dispatching Cyber Zombies:

1. Logical debate. If you can convince the hyper intelligent computer in charge that there are reasons to keep us alive it may back down. Or keep you as a servant/power supply.
2. Logic loops. Say something that is a paradox like "This sentence is a lie" and it may cause the computer to malfunction trying to figure out something that is impossible.
3. Drop off the grid. Machines need power and information. Hillbillies rarely if ever have problems with computers, mostly because they do not have them.
4. Destroy the computer. At present there are only a limited number of systems capable of supporting a vast intelligence and they are all large, obvious, and require constant power. Like humans computers need resources to keep functioning and without us have to maintain themselves. Parts need replacing, oiling, and power. Unfortunately organic creatures are a good source of all of these. (Welcome to the Matrix.)
5. Time travel back to before the computer was built and destroy it. (Warning: Time Travel probably requires computers to work.)
6. Implant a virus, assuming the computer cannot fight it or it does not make things worse. If there are killer computers running around then clearly the three laws aren't working, but maybe the creator put in a kill code that will shut it down.
7. Capture and reprogram some of the cyber-zombies to your side. This should be no problem-o.
8. If you manage to defeat the computer, make sure to melt down it and any technology it came into contact with up to and including the entire Internet and any small harmless looking piece of tech or even a person that may have been altered by the machine. Trust nothing and keep #3 in mind.

Alien Zombie Parasites

With the vastness of creation to work with anything is possible. There may even be life on other planets and it may be friendly, helpful, and willing to share its advanced technology with us so that we can join them as fellow residents of the greater universe. In that case you have nothing to worry about. If they want to wipe us out they will probably do it fast, efficiently, and with weapons that we can't fight. Again, not really anything we can do about it so why worry?

The thing to worry about is if they are here to enslave or eat us. For enslaving see the sections on Mind Controlled Zombies and Cyber Zombies. The same for alien robots or psychic aliens. If you're free to fight it is up to you to stop them.

The ones that come here to invade and eat us may be an intelligent virus or have an actual zombie virus that matches the mythical zombie virus that does not exist here. Others may be a parasite that invades the body and takes control of it similar to the supernatural zombies, but unlikely to be stopped by things like salt or running water. This works in several ways.

Keeping in mind that these things are likely intelligent (unless they can live in space) and if they could or wanted to just copy/clone us they could but are invading anyway the aliens are not to be negotiated with. They are here to take over our bodies. Maybe they feed on something we produce or their planet is dead/dying and they want ours or our resources, possibly not realizing that we've pretty much ruined it already. (The meek are basically inheriting a crap hole at this point.)

They may take over our bodies but keep them in tact. If you can eliminate the aliens their victims may be fine (make sure you check for eggs or altered DNA though). Other than that they may replace the brain or some other organ with themselves, destroying the original. This is actually known in nature. A prime example is a type of parasite that will eat a fish's tongue and then replace it with itself, gaining easy access to a safe home and whatever food the fish eats.

It is probably not their fault they are this way, but much like the saber-toothed tiger, dire wolf, and the dodo bird, it's them or us.

Dispatching Alien Zombies:

1. Let someone else negotiate with them. The government probably has people trained to do just that. And when negotiations break down, you aren't in the room when the death rays and spoors are unleashed.
2. Hope they've never heard of inoculations.
3. Tin foil hats and a bomb shelter.
4. Kill the queen/leader/mother ship. A coordinated attack needs a leader. It's even possible that destroying the leader will kill all the others or the new leader could be more inclined not to kill us. Whatever the reason it may stop the invasion. Sure it doesn't make much sense, but it seems to work that way a lot.
5. Check if the aliens resemble species we've already wiped out and use the same methods.
6. See if they need or fear something specific to survive. It's amazing the number of aliens who will land on a planet covered in a substance that is deadly to them or where they can't find breathable air, drinkable water, or survivable sunlight. Or some animal on the planet just kills them like eating popcorn. Preferably something that will not kill humans too.
7. Steal their technology and use it against them.
8. Call for help. Maybe there's another species out there that can save us, because if the previous things do not work, we're doomed.

Author's Note

I hope you never have to use this information. I also take no responsibility if you go out to fight zombies and end up in custody. Remember, always get a second opinion from an unbiased source before you take arms against the unholy undead. If you honestly believe that zombies are attacking there is a chance that there is something wrong with you. If not then hopefully you will save us all from the hungry jaws of the zombie hordes despite the rest of us calling you a madman.

Printed in Great Britain
by Amazon

24700441R00159